Bloody Twine #3
Twisted Tales with Twisted Endings
Matthew L. Marlott

This book is for all who just wish to sit back, relax, and enjoy some twisted tales with twisted endings. This book is dedicated to fans of traditional horror.
If you like this book, give it a good review and tell me what your favorite story was in this collection.

Table of Contents

Preface

These stories were originally published on my own personal site, bloodytwine.com. It's a little site that has received an equal amount of little attention, but it's mine, and I'm proud of it. I use this site to perfect my stories, and thanks to it, you have these bundles of fine short horror tales you can now peruse and enjoy at your leisure.

Imagine walking into an abandoned storage room filled with old newspapers and magazines, all articles stacked in bundles neatly tied with twine, but then you discover other bundles, bundles not so neatly tied, ragged bundles of yellowed and partially-charred paper tied in bloodstained twine.

You see, some stories are meant to educate, and some stories are meant to entertain, but some stories…some stories are simply looking for a victim.

Enjoy.

Bloody Twine #3

Both scenic and deadly.
Josie could make out the large jagged boulders dotted here and there within the circle, those boulders resting upon deep lines drawn in the sand, those lines spinning round to converge in the center of this weird piece of field art…
Average Read Time: 36m 54s

James and the giant breach.
Whenever a breach opened, it would scatter items from other universes along a conical path, and these "artifacts," no matter how mundane-looking, were always endowed with dimensional energy, making them worth their weight in gold. That's why the State wanted them, but James wasn't interested in what the State wanted, nor had he ever been…
Average Read Time: 48m 42s

It's retro-progressive!
He skirted around a number of dead bodies, students who had suddenly died from the bad time three weeks ago. He had dim memories before that time, memories of himself and Brittney in something called a "dorm," maybe an "apartment," but that life was a million years gone in his mind, so those memories no longer mattered…
Average Read Time: 13m 9s

Obey is a four-letter word.

He was fourteen now, but he was also the oldest in his class, just in front of Dasheena, who was a mere month younger than him. They were grouped by age, so Christoff was the leader of Class Three, and he was proud of that fact. He would not fail Mr. Jonas. He would not fail the Patriot School for Wayward Children. He would obey…

Average Read Time: 11m 45s

There is both madness and method to her scorn.

The screams around her were deafening, a screaming that bubbled up from the lake of fire that was split by this stone path, and she could see shapes in that lake, vaguely-human forms that reached and struggled for the surface…

Average Read Time: 18m 7s

T is for Terror.

This man, this "Yanosh," was indeed something terrifying. His face was gone; there were only bits of melted flesh hanging off of a white skull, two very human eyes looking out from the orbital sockets, his tongue hanging out of the right side of his mouth through a gap in his broken teeth…

Average Read Time: 16m 30s

It's horror in Fay English!

There were shops and houses here and there, but they all looked different in style and make from anything else she'd encountered in this state. There were cottages of stone walls and thatched roofs coupled by larger buildings of slate block, something old-fashioned and

foreign that did not represent the Midwest houses that normally dotted the landscape out here...
Average Read Time: 22m 5s

Hungry for a sale?
Dawn emerged from behind him as he drove west. The early-morning light emblazoned everything with its welcomed glow, so it was no surprise when the first of the road signs came into view. It wasn't the signs that distracted him, however. It was the singular house in the distance that caught his eye, a white two-story of brand-new build, a little gem out in the middle of nowhere...
Average Read Time: 13m 57s

When Hell freezes over.
Andy was twenty-five and just starting out, but he knew he had a bright future. In fact, things were already going his way. By some miracle of amazing fortune, no one had rented the incredibly-cheap bottom apartment in this little two-story, and the only other occupant in the building was an ancient crone of a woman that supposedly lived in the upstairs apartment, but he didn't know anything about her, nor did he need to...
Average Read Time: 40m 4s

How long can you hold your breath?
Scott was well familiar with Prisoner's Rock; everyone was. It was a large chunk of boulder-like land just jutting out of Prisoner's Creek, but nobody ever went out to it. There were a lot of stories attached to it, or rather, a lot of stories attached to what was next to it,

submerged next to it under the water. Nevertheless, Scott wasn't scared of some stupid local legends...
Average Read Time: 26m 15s

#1…ROCK GARDEN

Both scenic and deadly.

Josette stepped off the bus and onto the sidewalk of Engles. She balanced Houston on her hip as the toddler squirmed to look around the immediate vicinity. This little patch of dirt was far enough away that Jeremy wouldn't find her, and Josie was honestly surprised this place even had a bus stop.

An old man in a faded-blue denim shirt, rugged blue jeans on him, walked up and eyed her with mild suspicion.

"Josie?" he asked.

"Yeah…" smiled Josie.

"I'm Henry," replied the old man. "Henry Farnsworth. I'm your ride."

"Oh, good," said Josie. "I was afraid I'd have to call Carol again."

"She sent me up here to wait just in case," said Henry.

"Oh…" said Josie in uncomfortable reply. "I hope you didn't wait too long."

"Only an hour," smiled the old man.

"Oh…" said Josie in yet another uncomfortable reply.

The old man, Henry, bent down and gave Houston a smile.

"So this is the little pup, huh?" he said. "It's been many a year since Carol and I have had a little one in the house."

"Oh, we won't be any trouble," said Josie nervously. "I promise I'll help around the house…"

"Oh, don't you worry 'bout that," grinned Henry. "Now, I'm not being rude, so don't take offense, but we have to go, so let's get a move on. Carol's got a room all set up for you, and she's eager to meet you two."

"Okay…" replied Josie.

She followed the kindly gentleman as he traveled down the street to a nearby parking lot. He walked up to a large red truck and motioned her around to the other side.

"Carol went ahead and bought one of those car seats for the little one," said Henry. "You'll just have to squeeze him in back there. It's a tight fit inside here, but he'll be just fine in the backseat."

"Oh…" said Josie. "Thank you."

She buckled in Houston and then took to the front passenger seat. It was indeed a tight fit, but that was more than fine, because she had not expected such hospitality from two strangers, and she did not want to screw up this whole arrangement.

Her friend, Loren, a middle-aged woman that had worked with her at a dollar store—that store Josie's former place of employment—Loren had set this whole thing up, and it was turning out far better than Josie had originally estimated.

They drove through the small town of Engles after that, though there really was nothing much to see. It was a small town like any other but significantly smaller, so what Josie was going to do out here to pass the time was already in question, and she didn't even have a phone anymore for obvious reasons. She did not want Jeremy tracking her.

None of this would have happened had Dave not abandoned them. He had just up and disappeared a couple of weeks back, and then Josie had started receiving threatening phone calls from Jeremy and his crew. That meth-dealing thug had first demanded where Dave was, but that had stopped a few days ago. Now Jeremy was threatening her about money, so whatever was going on, whatever Dave had gotten into, was enough for Josie to pick up and leave with Houston.

Dave had said that he had come into some money, that he was going to take all three of them to live somewhere better, but that had turned out to be fiction. It was clear now that Houston's father had taken whatever money he'd come across and run, leaving Josie and their son to fend for themselves.

Without a second income, she couldn't afford to pay the rent for the trailer they'd been living in, and coupled with threats from Jeremy and his crew, there was nothing else left to do but run. So, this little deal she had worked out with Loren was better than nothing, though she did not relish the thought of living with strangers for a while. Now she and Houston were here in Engles, riding to who-knew-where in some stranger's truck.

Henry made small talk as they drove through the surrounding countryside, but other than fields of corn and soybeans with some cattle dotted here and there, there was not much else out here, out here in the country away from anything city-worthy.

The elderly Mr. Farnsworth seemed to know what was on her mind.

"It's nice and quiet out here," said Henry. "You'll find the occasional drunken brawl in town, maybe some petty theft, but us folks out here don't have much to worry about come any danger-like. It's a good place to retire, though I can see how young folks would get an itch'un to leave. Yeah, Engles is pretty small, so the bus stop's mainly for people leaving it, not coming to it."

"Uh, huh…" said Josie uncertainly.

"Our property is a good place, though," explained Henry. "Owned that farm for as long as Carol and I have been married, though we don't actually farm it anymore. It's a real nice place for walking and hiking, but there are a few rules to follow."

"Rules?" asked Josie.

She wasn't too keen on taking orders, but these people had been kind enough to take in her and Houston, so a few rules were okay for the time being.

"They're for your own safety," explained Henry. "We don't keep pigs, cattle, or horses anymore—too much work for us old folks—so there's no danger there, but there are wild animals around the neighboring woods that can be a problem. Coyotes, mainly, but they can be extremely dangerous in packs, especially for a little one like Houston."

"Oh," replied Josie. "We had raccoons back where I lived, but they were mainly a nuisance."

"They're still a nuisance," chuckled Henry. "We have old Pete to drive them off, but don't worry about him. He's a good dog, and he likes kids, so you don't have to worry about him."

"Oh, that's good," said Josie.

"There's the old shed out back that has our work tools," said Henry. "That's got a lot of old sharp equipment, some of it rusty, so you'll want to avoid that."

"Okay," replied Josie.

Henry grew quiet for a moment, so Josie looked over to him for a brief inspection, but the old man's weathered face darkened as a serious look washed over him.

"Then there's the Circle," he said quietly.

"The Circle?" asked Josie.

"Yeah…" frowned Henry. "Just…stay away from it."

"Okay," said Josie in obvious confusion. "I…I mean…uhhh…what…am I…staying away from?"

"The Circle is out in a field on our property," said Henry. "You'd know it if you saw it, and you will see it…It's impossible to miss…It's all white sand smoothed out in spiraling circles, and there are a bunch of large rocks in it…boulders, I'd guess you'd call 'em…Just…stay away from it."

"Okay," replied Josie. "Is it…like…a pet project of yours?"

"No," said Henry, and there was a tinge of resentment mixed with bitterness in his old voice. "No, it is not. In fact, I'd get rid of it if I could, but that's not going to happen. There's no telling what would happen if I tried to do that. Best just to plant trees around it again. Never should have cut down those trees in the first place."

"I…see…" said Josie in more confusion.

"It's dangerous," said Henry. "Just trust me when I say that, and stay away from it…and don't let the little one anywhere near it, understand?"

"Okay," breathed out Josie. "I mean, I'm not—"

But she was cut short.

"I'm not joking," said Henry in a deadly serious tone. "Keep an eye on your boy when you're out there. It's nice to walk around the property, but just…stay away from the Circle. Don't let him anywhere near it."

"Will do," nodded Josie.

Henry was strangely quiet after that, but the drive to the old couple's residence did not take long, and that was good, because Josie was left wondering just exactly what it was she had stumbled into.

*****

Josie sat down next to Carol in one of the elderly woman's old-fashioned, outdoor wooden chairs.

She smoothed the creases out of her new white-and-blue print dress—the dress white with blue-print flowers—mainly because she did not want to get it dirty. She was not used to wearing dresses, but the old woman had given her several upon arrival, so she had felt compelled to wear them, at least for today, if only out of courtesy.

"You're not used to wearing dresses, are you, dear?" asked Carol.

"No, ma'am," said Josie nervously. "It's blue jeans and T-shirts where I come from."

"Well, there's nothing wrong with being a little old-fashioned every once in a while," said the old woman. "You'll get used to it."

"What I'm not used to is…uhhh…this," said Josie.

She motioned toward the large wooden container before her that was currently filled with cream, that container a butter churn, the cream inside ready to be churned.

Carol gripped the plunger of her own butter churn and nodded once at Josie's.

"It's not difficult to learn," she smiled. "It can be hard on your hands, and it will leave you tired, but you'll get used to it."

The old woman took to churning with her plunger, and Josie tried to imitate her as best she could.

"We don't raise cows anymore," said Carol. "Nope, we don't have any cattle anymore, so we get our cream from our neighbors down the road."

"Why is it that all country folk churn butter?" asked Josie. "I thought that was just a trope on TV and in the movies."

Carol laughed and shook her head no.

"I don't know about that," she chuckled, "but most people don't do this. I took it up as a way to pass the time. It gives me something to do when I'm not quilting, and the exercise is good for me…but it's not something that everyone in the country does…

"It's like riding horses. Everyone from the big city thinks we ride horses everywhere. We had horses years ago, but we don't have them anymore, and a lot of folks 'round here don't, either. Too expensive to care for."

"Oh…" said Josie as she turned a mild shade of red. "I didn't know."

They continued to work at churning their cream, and Josie silently admitted to herself that it was new and interesting to do this particular activity, if not tiring. It was like being at some kind of old-fashioned farm camp.

"I had a horse when I was younger," nodded Carol, a slight smile on her face. "His name was Outlaw, probably the most overused name ever for a stallion, but I loved him so. I rode him I don't know how many days out in these back fields, but I lost him one night when he escaped the stable. Someone forgot to lock it…probably me. He got out and wandered too close to the…the…N…Never mind that…He died in an accident, and I've had other horses, but they never matched up to him."

Carol's face darkened at the mention of her beloved horse's death, and this made Josie curious, but she did not want to press the old woman on the matter, so she swiftly changed topics.

"So…quick question…" said Josie nervously. "Umm…What are we going to do with all this butter?"

Carol laughed and shook her head in amusement.

"Yeah, there's a little more than we can use here," she said. "I actually tub it up and sell it down at the local grocery store. I keep a tub for myself, but…you know how that is. Unless you're making cakes, you don't really need a ton of butter."

"Yeah…heh…" said Josie. "I figured it was something like that."

It was Carol's turn to suddenly change topics, and she nodded toward Houston in attention of the toddler. The little boy was sitting on the porch while sifting through a variety of shiny glass beads and various colored buttons that Carol had given him, the toddler sorting them out into their respective piles of similarities.

"I was afraid to give him those," said the old woman. "You know how little ones are, but you said this is what he likes to do."

"Yeah…" nodded Josie. "He won't try to swallow any of them."

"Houston doesn't talk much, does he?" asked Carol in slight confusion. "I don't think I've heard him speak up a lot."

"Houston's autistic," explained Josie. "He's on the spectrum, so he doesn't talk a lot. He likes to do what he likes to do, and sorting things is a favorite of his."

"Oh," said Carol in strange interest. "I didn't know."

"It's okay," shrugged Josie. "There's a lot of misinformation on autism, but I'm learning about it."

"Well, that's good," nodded Carol. "You've got to look after your own. We watched our daughter, Gloria, like a hawk after Henry Jr…Can't be too careful."

"Henry Jr?" asked Josie.

She had asked the question without thinking, not realizing what effect it could have.

Carol grimaced and shook her head no at the query.

"He…disappeared," frowned the old woman. "He was only five. Went wandering out of his bed at night and left the house…Just vanished. Everyone around here searched everywhere for him, but they never found a trace of him."

"Oh…" said Josie with wide eyes.

"That was…oh…forty-five years ago now," said Carol. "Time dulls the pain after a while, but you never forget…No, you never forget."

Josie had no response to this. She had not expected to hear of terrible tragedy while churning butter, so she said nothing.

They continued with their task for several minutes after that without saying anything, and it was awkward, so Josie did her best just to lose herself in the work.

She would have continued on like this were it not for the loud barking of a dog in the distance. That barking jerked her head up from her appointed task, mainly because it had startled her out of her own stewed worries.

"What is that all about…?" she asked, but then she noticed something far more important.

Houston was not in visible sight anymore. There were only two piles of correctly separated beads and buttons where the little boy had once been.

"Houston?" asked Josie in instant panic. "Houston!"

She stopped churning, stood, and looked this way and that for any sign of him.

"Come on," said Carol in a firm, commanding voice.

The old woman stood up and quickly walked to the end of the porch, walking toward the sound of the barking dog.

"That's old Pete," said Carol with a strange conviction in her tone. "He doesn't bark for no reason."

Josie followed the elderly woman out to the back field, trying not to let her panic overwhelm her.

"Houston!" she called out. "Houston!"

The old woman in front of her made a beeline for the distant barking, so Josie followed her without question.

They made their way through the knee-high grass to the dog, a big red mutt with a pinkish nose, and the old dog immediately bounded toward them in both greeting and urgency.

"What is it, boy?" asked Carol.

Josie could see slight movement in the grass ahead, and then she spied the brown hair of her only child, so she rushed forward to get him. Houston was sitting in the grass, but he appeared unharmed, so she scooped him up without further thought or ado.

"What were you doing?" she breathed out. "You can't run off like that! It's dangerous..."

She looked up but stopped speaking as she noticed the area they were next to, this new, unnoticed feature of the field a mere twenty feet away. There was a large circle ahead of them, a very large circle, a great big circle of white sand that spanned about a hundred feet in diameter.

Josie could make out the large jagged boulders dotted here and there within the circle, those boulders resting upon deep lines drawn in the sand, those lines spinning round to converge in the center of this weird piece of field art.

She felt a strange sense of foreboding rest upon her, as if she were in imminent danger, though she could not put her finger on why.

Carol walked up to her from behind, so Josie turned to address her, but the old woman did not look happy.

"We have to keep a better eye on him," said Carol. "It's a good thing old Pete said something."

"I'm sorry about this..." began Josie.

"Don't apologize to me," said Carol as she shook her head no. "You didn't know. I know how it is to get distracted by work, but it's too dangerous to let the little one just wander off."

"I...I know..." said Josie. "I...I thought..."

"It doesn't matter," said Carol with another shake of her head. "Let's just get away from here and back to the house. We need to go back. We don't come out here, and we're too close to the Circle, way too close. That's why Pete was barking."

She turned around after that and started back toward the farmhouse, a sense of finality in her firm tone.

The big red dog, Pete, did not follow Carol back. He simply stared at Josie with big brown eyes and whined, unmoving from his sitting position, as if he were waiting for Josie to move before taking off, himself.

Josie did not know what to make of any of it, but she was a guest here, so she would do as ordered.

She started back toward the farmhouse when the sound of a crow startled her. She turned back to look for the bird, and she spied the ugly black thing as it perched upon one of the boulders in the so-called "Circle."

Josie shook her head and continued back toward the house, Houston balanced on her hip. She was already agitated because of what had just happened, and some stupid bird was not going to agitate her further, or so she thought.

She heard a loud squawk in the distance, not the normal cawing of a crow, and she turned to look back toward the Circle, but the ugly black bird was gone. There were a couple of feathers floating through the air where it had just been perching and nothing else, no other trace of it.

"What the…?" she whispered to herself.

"Josie!" called out Carol from the distance.

"Coming!" called back Josie.

She hurried back to the farmhouse, but the whole incident with Houston had shaken her, and she was going to have to question her generous hosts about this "Circle," because if the strange work of field art truly was dangerous, she wanted to know why.

*****

Josie sat down for dinner at the Farnsworth's family dinner table. She had helped Carol cook, though she, herself, was not much of one. Nevertheless, she had managed to learn quite a bit during the time it had taken to make their nightly meal.

Houston was in an old wooden highchair that had been generously provided by Carol, something the elderly woman had stored away a long time ago and had never disposed of. The little boy sat next to his mother while eating select bits of boneless chicken breast off his plate, because Carol had insisted on feeding him first.

Josie sensed that the adults were not supposed to eat yet, so she waited patiently for her hosts to give the okay.

The old man, Henry, closed his eyes and clasped his hands in prayer.

Josie did not know what to do, so she simply listened.

"Lord…" said the old man. "Lord, thank you for this bounty you have bestowed upon us, and thank you for watching over our guests today. Please, continue to protect your faithful children from the darkness that lurks ever near us…Amen."

"Amen," repeated Josie.

His prayer seemed rather disturbing to her, though she did not have the nerve to ask him about it. However, that didn't mean she wouldn't eventually broach the topic.

They ate for a few minutes before Josie decided to ask anything, though she knew what she wanted to ask was probably a source of contention.

"I…I have a question," she said nervously.

The elderly couple stared at each other with a knowing, worried look, but it was Carol who spoke up for the both of them. The old woman turned her anxious gaze upon Josie and gave her a slight frown.

"You want to know about the Circle," said Carol.

"Y…Yes…" replied Josie.

"It's dangerous—" started Henry, but Carol shushed him.

"She already knows that," said the old woman. "We should tell her everything."

"Okay…" sighed Henry. "Have it your way."

Carol frowned, shook her head, and then turned her attention back upon Josie.

"The Circle has been here since the natives lived on this land," said Carol. "Where it came from or who made it, I've never been able to find out. In fact, we didn't even know it existed until we bought the land from the Sutherlands, back when we were newlyweds."

"Oh…" said Josie. "But…you can clearly see it. You can probably see it from satellite pictures…Why hasn't anybody ever heard of it?"

"All of this area was thick woodland back in the day," explained Henry. "We cut down those trees to make space for planting…That's when we discovered it."

"The Sutherlands never warned us about the Circle," said Carol. "We…learned that the hard way."

"Why?" asked Josie in confusion. "Why is it dangerous? It just looks like a neat, rock-garden-type place."

"That it does," said Henry. "It's fairly safe during the day, but—"

"You don't go anywhere near it at night," nodded Carol.

"Why?" asked Josie. "I don't understand…I mean, who maintains it? You must have to fix it after it rains…"

Her sentence died in her throat as Henry shook his head no.

"Those circles out there?" he asked. "Those ruts in the sand? We don't have anything to do with that."

"Then how—?" began Josie, but Carol answered that question rather abruptly.

"It's the stones," nodded the old woman. "They move at night. They're asleep during the day."

Josie had to do a doubletake for her ears. She was not quite sure she'd heard right.

"Excuse me, what?" she asked in surprise.

"The boulders out there move," said Henry. "It's hard to believe, I know, but it's the truth. If you go out there tomorrow, you'll see…They'll all be in different places."

"I've kept a log over the years," said Carol. "I'm not good with sketches, but those stones…they move in patterns. I don't know what it means, but…they're never in the same place twice in a row."

"And the sand there?" asked Henry. "We don't know where that comes from."

"We really don't," shrugged Carol. "It's just always been there, and it never seems to get washed away by rain, even in downpours."

"Uh, huh," said Josie with wide eyes. "If all of that's true, then why haven't you shown other people? You could make a lot of money off of tourism with something like that."

"It's too dangerous," said Henry firmly.

"But why is it dangerous?" asked Josie. "I know plenty of people that would like to see it."

"No," said Carol with a shake of her head. "Anything that goes into that circle isn't coming out again. You might be able to safely enter it during the day, but you won't get out alive once nightfall hits."

"Oh…" said Josie uncertainly.

It occurred to her that her hosts, though both nice and generous, were clearly crazy. She wondered, however, if their insanity was only limited to the Circle story or if it ran deeper than that.

"You know that horse I told you about?" asked Carol. "Outlaw, my favorite horse I had when I was young?...I found his body out by the Circle. His head was gone. There was one of those boulders in front of poor Outlaw, but there was never any sign of his head. He got out of the stable one night and...that was all that was left of him the next morning."

"Oh, wow," breathed Josie. "We'll...uhhh...We'll stay away from the Circle, then."

"That's the smart decision," nodded Carol. "Henry is going to replant trees around that cursed place this year. I'm sure you can help us with that, right? That should hide the Circle again...We should have never cut down those trees around it in the first place...You can help us replant some trees, right?"

"Sure," nodded Josie. "Sure, I can help you with that."

But she had no intention of helping them with that. No, Josie's only intent was to find somewhere else to hide from Jeremy and his crew, because this old couple, nice as they were, were both nuttier than a peanut bar, and that meant they weren't exactly safe to be around.

*****

Josie exited Henry's truck and gave him a reassuring, if false, smile.

"I'll be right back," she said as she unstrapped Houston from his car seat.

"Take your time," smiled Henry. "I don't mind waiting."

"Thank you," said Josie. "I'll just be a minute."

She scooped up Houston, shut the truck door, and walked to the entrance of the little convenience store they had parked next to.

She was going to have to get someone to lend her their phone, because she needed to make other arrangements for somewhere to stay. The Farnsworths…were not going to work out.

Josie walked into the convenience store and looked around for anyone who seemed even vaguely trustworthy. She spied a couple, a middle-aged gentleman and a young lady who looked to be in her early twenties, and one look at them quickly convinced her that they had to be a father/daughter pair.

Josie walked up to them as the pair perused an aisle stocked with cans of soup and other such goods.

"Excuse me," she said quickly. "I don't have a phone, and I really need to make a call. Could I borrow your phone for a second? I need my sister to come and pick me up."

The pair took one look at her and Houston and immediately acquiesced. Having a small child with you did have some advantages.

"Here," said the young lady. "You can use mine."

The young woman unlocked her smartphone and handed it over.

Josie smiled in return and quickly dialed the number she had memorized as a last resort, and this was indeed a last resort. Most people didn't know phone numbers off the tops of their heads anymore, but Josie had this one down, and it was definitely, one-thousand-percent, a last resort.

The phone rang a couple of times before it was picked up, which was a miracle in itself, because she had been fairly certain Caitlyn would not pick up an unknown number.

"Hello?" asked Josie's younger sister on the other end of the line.

"Caitlyn?" asked Josie.

"Josie?" asked her sister. "Where have you been? I haven't heard anything from you…It's like you just disappeared."

"I had a friend from work set me up with a place," said Josie. "It's not working out, though."

"That sucks," said Caitlyn. "What happened?"

"I'll tell you in a minute," said Josie. "I need someone to pick me up from here, because I'm not taking the bus again."

"Where is 'here'?" asked Caitlyn.

"I'm in a little town called Engles," said Josie. "I'm staying with an old couple, the Farnsworths. They're nice people, but…they're a little crazy. I'm not sure it's safe to stay with them."

"Why are you out there?" asked Caitlyn. "Never mind. I already know why…Why didn't you just go back to Mom and Dad?"

"No…" said Josie firmly. "I can't go back there. I can't do that…Look, can you pick me up or not?"

"I'll pick you up," said Caitlyn, "but where are you going to go?"

"I'll figure something out," said Josie. "Please, just come and get me."

"I'll be there as soon as I can," sighed Caitlyn. "This place isn't out of state, is it?"

"No," replied Josie.

"Good," said Caitlyn. "Because I really don't want to make an interstate trip."

"It's not that far," said Josie. "It doesn't matter…Look, I've got to go. I've got someone waiting for me. I'll talk more about it when you get here."

"Okay," sighed Caitlyn. "See you when I get there."

Josie ended the call, gave the young lady back her phone, and walked back out of the convenience store, Houston in hand. She had not wanted to call Caitlyn, but her younger sister was the only option she had left, so that was that.

She returned to Henry's truck, strapped in Houston, and took to the front passenger seat.

"All finished?" asked the old man. "Did you find what you were looking for?"

"No," sighed Josie. "They were all out. I'll try again later."

"Oh," said Henry. "That's a shame."

"Yeah," replied Josie. "It really is."

She did not like lying to the kindly old man, but at the same time, she did not feel the Farnsworths were entirely safe to be around.

*****

Josie walked with Houston balanced on her hip, trudging along with him through the field next to the Farnsworth's home. She wanted to take one last look at this so-called "Circle" before her sister arrived.

She had not informed the elderly couple that she would be leaving, but she would think of something once Caitlyn showed up. She felt bad about giving them the runaround with this; they had been truly generous to her, but she had that feeling in her gut that things weren't exactly what they appeared to be at this homestead.

She threw those anxious thoughts aside as she walked toward the Circle.

She got within ten feet of the strange, overgrown rock garden before stopping, because though she had the urge to enter it and look around, that old superstitious fear caused by peer pressure forced her to hesitate.

She did not like to be bullied by superstition, something she had always considered ridiculous, but then she noticed something that would normally be impossible without major cooperation from numerous people, and this only added to her hesitation.

"What the…?" she breathed out.

The boulders, all of varying sizes, widths, and weights, were indeed in different places, but she wasn't entirely sure.

"That can't be right," she frowned. "This has to be my imagination."

She could swear they had all moved several feet counterclockwise, because she remembered the previous location of the big boulder where the crow had landed, but all of the rocks were still evenly spread out, so that couldn't be right…It couldn't be.

Josie took her time walking around the giant work of field art, but she did not get far before she spied the corpse of a dead animal, or at least, what was left of one.

Half of a racoon, the back half, was right outside of the Circle, the front half gone…just gone…with flies buzzing around the open meat of what was left.

Josie walked up and inspected the dead animal, but the stench of it drove her back a bit. In front of the thing was a smaller boulder, one on the outer edge of the Circle, but other than that, there was nothing else nearby except field grass and dirt.

She had a strange fear strike her, that fear of the unnatural, so she slowly backed away, turned, and headed back toward the house. Whatever was going on here was too much for her, and whether or not the Farnsworths were crazy, this place was starting to spook her in more ways than one.

*****

Josie stood out on the porch with Carol, Houston in hand. Henry was currently in the house, and old Pete was somewhere off in the neighboring woods, so it was now just the three of them, a trio of figures with a backdrop of an old country farmhouse that would have looked good in a painting.

The sun was setting, and its descent behind the eastern trees was quite beautiful, something scenic in a rustic environment that Josie was not used to. She held onto Houston as she viewed it, breathless at the sight of it.

The old woman must have noticed Josie's expression, because she commented upon it a moment later.

"It's beautiful, isn't it?" asked Carol. "It can get lonely out in the country sometimes, but when you have all of this around you, the natural beauty of it all, it makes it all worthwhile."

But this astute observation only heightened Josie's guilt about leaving.

"Yeah…" she said unhappily.

"What's wrong, hon?" asked the old woman.

Josie felt that twinge of regret stab into her. She needed to say something about how this situation wasn't working out, but she also didn't want to hurt the old couple's feelings.

"It's just that…" she began, but she stopped as she viewed lights in the distance.

Someone was driving down the old gravel road that led here, here to this property out in the middle of nowhere.

"I wonder who that could be?" asked Carol absentmindedly.

But something was wrong. There was more than one set of vehicle lights on the way, at least three pairs, something Josie had not been expecting.

Henry stepped from out of the doorway of the house and walked up next to them.

"We have visitors?" he asked.

A black truck and two old cars pulled up to the house, and Josie's eyes went wide as she finally realized what was going on.

"Oh, no…" she said under her breath.

They stepped out of the vehicles, Jeremy and his crew, and Josie knew she was in trouble. She could not even call the police…She didn't have her phone with her.

There were all five of his thugs with him, Brayce, Eric, Donovan, Josh, and Lorn, all five of them the scum of the earth as far as Josie was concerned.

Even worse…Caitlyn was with them.

Caitlyn was pushed forward by Jeremy, and Josie could tell in the fading light that her sister was crying…Her younger sister had bruises on her face.

Caitlyn cried out as Jeremy shoved her to the ground. He pointed a pistol at Josie and her elderly hosts as he kicked over Caitlyn, the young woman crying out in pain as she fell flat to her face in the dirt.

"Did you think I wouldn't find you!" he shouted.

"Hey, now!" started Henry, but he stopped his forward progression as Jeremy pointed his gun at him.

"You stop right there, old man!" yelled Jeremy.

The other five with him withdrew their own handguns and walked forward to match his position in a line right in front of the house, right before the porch.

Caitlyn whined and quietly sobbed from her prone position in the dirt, and Josie wanted to help her, but her first thought was for the safety of Houston.

She clutched her little boy tightly to her as Jeremy stared her down.

The young man adjusted his backwards ball cap and pointed his pistol at her.

"Where's my money, Jose!" he asked, and his tone was not friendly.

"I…I don't…" stammered Josie.

Jeremy planted his booted right foot onto the back-right pocket of Caitlyn's blue jeans and pushed down into her bottom. Caitlyn shrieked out again in protest, and the sound of her pain cut through Josie like a chainsaw.

"I'm not going to ask again!" yelled Jeremy.

"D…Dave ran off with it!" sputtered Josie. "He'd said he'd gotten some money, but he abandoned me and Houston, took the money, and ran! Why do you think I'm out here! I have nowhere else to go!"

She didn't want to cry, but she felt tears spill from her eyes anyway.

"Dave?" asked Jeremy. "Seriously?"

He laughed as the rest of his crew joined in with him.

"That junkie didn't have the money," he said with a cruel grin. "And he didn't 'abandon' you."

"What?" asked Josie in confusion.

"Where do you think he went?" asked Jeremy. "He was stealing meth, my meth, and he was pocketing the cash off of what he was selling. Then, he had the grain to go and steal every last penny from the vault…That's right…He made off with our shipment fund…That's fifty-K, sweetheart…Nobody robs us…Nobody…But he won't be stealing from us anymore…Who do you think buried him?"

Josie's lips turned downwards in both shock and anguish over this realization.

"You…You killed him?" she choked out.

The group of six laughed once more.

"No one's going to miss that meth-head," said Jeremy. "The only ones who will miss him are his trailer-trash girlfriend and his retard kid…Now, I know he gave you the money, Jose, and I want my money. Don't make me tell you again."

He pointed the barrel of his gun toward the back of Caitlyn's blonde head.

"No, wait!" cried Josie.

The sun finally set behind the trees in the distance, and lights on various poles automatically turned on around the farm as darkness flooded over them.

"One last chance, Jose," said Jeremy.

"I don't know about any mon—" began Josie, but she was cut short.

"I know where it is!" spoke up Henry.

Josie looked over at the old man in surprise. There was no way he could possibly know where that money had gone.

"Is that right, old man?" asked Jeremy.

"Yeah, young feller," said Henry in defiance. "Now you just hold your horses there. That money you want is buried out back."

"Oh, really?" asked Jeremy.

"Yeah," frowned Henry. "You just need a shovel. It's out back. There're the farm lights out there, so it's easy enough to find."

"Right," frowned Jeremy in return. "You'd better not be lying to me, old man."

He turned and directed one of his crew, Lorn, toward the back of the black truck.

"Get the shovels," he said firmly.

Lorn stuffed his gun back into his jeans, walked to the truck, took two shovels out of the truck bed, and walked back with them.

"Everybody, get moving!" yelled Jeremy. "That means all of you!...You lead the way, old man."

He reached down and pulled up Caitlyn by her dyed-blonde hair. The young woman shrieked as she was forced to stand, and Jeremy pushed her forward without mercy.

"All of you, move it!" ordered Jeremy as he waved on Josie and her two elderly hosts.

Josie's heart pounded in her chest as she followed Henry and Carol out around the house, Caitlyn, Jeremy, and the rest of Jeremy's thug crew following closely behind.

Jeremy was probably going to kill them all, and there was nothing she could do about it. The only thing Josie could think of was to run toward the nearby woods, but she'd be running with Houston in hand, which would make it more difficult for them to escape without getting shot.

She held a faint hope that Henry had already thought of this, that the tree line was where he was leading them all, but this was not the case.

Henry continued walking out through the back field, walking with a stiff purpose, that purpose directed solely at the Circle. The farm lights on the outlying poles shone down upon the ominous, overgrown rock garden, lighting it up for all to see.

"Where are you going, old man?" snarled Jeremy.

"It's just up ahead," replied Henry. "It's in the middle of those boulders there."

"Is that right?" asked Jeremy.

The group walked up to the Circle and stopped right before it.

Henry waved one hand out toward the center of it.

"Buried it right in the middle there," he said firmly. "You can all go out there and see for yourself."

"Uh, huh," said Jeremy, his voice rife with suspicion.

He walked up and pushed Josie forward from behind. She cried out as she stumbled forward, but she stopped and regained her balance just before reaching the line of white sand that constituted the edge of the Circle.

"You go in first," growled the young man.

"What?" asked Josie. "But I—"

Jeremy pointed his gun at the back of Caitlyn's head, and the young blonde cried out in fear.

"Do it!" yelled Jeremy. "Do it, or you'll be wearing your sister's brains as a sweater."

Josie shook as she started to hand over Houston to Carol, but Jeremy stopped her.

"Uh, uh," said the gun-wielding thug. "He goes with you."

Henry walked over to her and nodded once.

"You just walk right on in to the center," he said confidently. "Once they see it's safe, then you can come right back. Just avoid the rocks, and you'll have no problems."

He handed something over to Houston while petting the little boy's head, and then he pressed something into Josie's free right hand.

Josie stared down at the small stone in her hand, and Houston held up a similar one, inspecting it as if he did not have a care in the world.

"You know how you feed the little one first?" asked Henry under his breath. "You always feed him first. You don't take food from him. We don't take food from our little ones. An adult won't take food from a little one."

Josie had no idea what the old man was going on about, so she wiped at her eyes and simply nodded yes in reply. It was becoming clearer and clearer to her that the elderly couple was just crazy, and unfortunately, that was of absolutely no help right now.

"Quit talking!" growled Jeremy. "Get moving, Jose! I want my money!"

Josie's tears continued to flow as she stepped into the Circle and onto white sand.

She stepped over the deep ruts in the sand as she headed for the center of the Circle. There was something about Henry's warning about not touching the boulders that stuck with her, so she continued on toward the center while walking around the large rocks.

A low rumble occurred beneath her feet, a vibration of sorts, and she could actually feel the sand shift beneath her a bit, but what this meant, she did not know.

"Keep going!" yelled Jeremy.

Josie winced as she felt a slight pain in her right hand. The small stone in her hand felt slightly hot, and it began to get hotter as she walked toward the center of the Circle. She looked over to Houston, but her little boy just kept switching his stone from one hand to the other, studying it with an intensity he had never shown before with any other ordinary rocks.

Josie opened her right hand and looked down at the stone resting in her palm.

The skin of her right hand was turning red where the stone rested, and she felt as if it were burning her, but she held onto it, because Henry's instructions were all she actually had to hold onto when it came to making it out of this situation alive. The old man had to have a plan, something he'd thought of, or he wouldn't have led them all out here, and these stones had something to do with it.

Josie stopped in the center of the Circle, this huge circle of spiraling white sand dotted with ominous-looking boulders, and she looked back toward the armed group of thugs, wondering what was next in Henry's plan, hoping desperately that the old man knew something that would save, at the very least, her little boy.

"It's right there!" called Henry. "It's right where you're standing! You asked me to bury it, and that's where it is!"

"All right!" yelled Jeremy. "Get back here!"

Josie walked back through the Circle, wary of touching any of the large boulders around her, but by the time she had made it back to the edge, her right hand was throbbing with a burning pain.

She stepped out of the Circle and quickly tossed her small stone back to the white sand behind her.

Houston continued to switch his stone from one little hand to the next, and she knew he would be reluctant to give it up, so she did not try to take it from him. She did not need a scene, not right now.

She stared down at her right hand to briefly inspect the large, bleeding, red welt on her palm, that welt covered with a fine coating of white sand. She ignored the pain of it as she brushed that sand off on her jeans, intent on hiding this little fact from prying eyes.

Something very strange was going on with these stones, something dangerous, something horrendous even, and there was an inkling in her of what that might be, but if that were true, impossible as it seemed, then Henry did indeed have a plan to get rid of Jeremy and his crew, and that plan was a permanent one.

"All right, everyone!" yelled Jeremy. "Let's grab the money and go!"

He waved everyone forward but gave a nod toward Brayce.

"Stay back and watch them," he said. "The old man couldn't have buried the money very deep. This won't take long."

Brayce turned and pointed his pistol at them as the others walked into the Circle.

Jeremy grabbed a shovel from Lorn and walked in with the rest of them.

"Let's get this done!" he yelled.

They all walked into the Circle toward the center, Jeremy and the other four, and they did not stop until they were at the place where Josie had just been.

"It's time to get some payback," said Jeremy.

He took his shovel and drove the blade into the sand, right in the center of the Circle, and with the driving in of that blade, the mayhem began.

Josie jumped a little as she heard the high-pitched, shrill scream of Donovon, a scream so unlike a man that it curdled her blood, but she could not look past the startled figure of Brayce to see what was going on.

"Hey, what!" yelled Brayce as he turned around toward the Circle, pistol raised and ready.

Henry took that opportunity to ambush Brayce from behind, pushing the young man forward with a rough and forceful shove. Brayce stumbled forward to land on his hands and knees within the first ring of the Circle, and then something happened that Josie would have never believed if she hadn't seen it with her own two eyes.

Brayce raised himself up on his arms in an attempt to stand, but a large boulder slid through the sand on its own accord and ran over both of his legs. The huge rock did not stop sliding, moving as if pushed by an invisible force as it traveled along the concentric rut that circled inwards toward the center.

Brayce screamed as blood spurted out from the two stumps that were left of his legs, that sanguine life spilling out to stain the white of the sand beneath him. He raised his left hand in reflex as another boulder sped toward him, and then he was gone, a slight stain of red on white sand as more white sand billowed out from beneath the boulder that had run him down, sand billowing out from it like a miniature desert storm.

Josie watched in horror as the boulders of this giant rock garden traveled in a circle along the ruts in the sand, speeding along as if by a will of their own.

She heard Josh screech in pain from somewhere on the other side of the Circle. She could see him off to her right, blood spraying from his missing right arm, the young man staggering in shock and terror, and then a speeding boulder ran him down, nothing left of him after that but sand, billowing sand where he had once been.

Her attention was taken by the screaming figure of Eric running toward them, though the gun-wielding thug only made it about ten feet. The young man tripped and fell as he stumbled over a rut, and then a boulder ran right through him, not over him but through him, and there was only half a torso with legs left after that, his intestines spilling out onto the sand, and even that torso vanished as another boulder took what was left.

Lorn dropped his shovel and bolted, but he was immediately run over. His head popped off like a cork as his entire body disappeared beneath a particularly large boulder. Josie could actually make out the surprised expression upon his face as his head rolled to a stop in one of the inner ruts. Another boulder ran over that head a second later, and then Lorn's head was gone too, disappearing in a burst of white sand.

Jeremy screamed as he dropped his shovel and pulled forth his gun from the back of his jeans. He fired around himself in wild abandon as he screeched out a curse, firing at the speeding rocks moving in a circle toward the center, ever toward the center.

Josie ducked down along with Henry, Carol, and Caitlyn as shots rang out in the night. She clutched Houston closely to her as she kept low, praying no bullets would strike them, especially her son.

"Head down, baby!" she choked out as she held him tightly.

But she did not follow her own advice.

Josie looked up to see Jeremy scream one last time as the various boulders within the Circle closed in on him like a vice, all of those large rocks attracted to the center as if pulled there by some kind of gigantic, supernatural magnet.

A fountain of blood sprayed up as the boulders converged upon the center, and then the heavy stones moved away from that center in a clockwise motion, moving away from a center of concentric circles with nothing in it, not even the shovel Jeremy had brought with him.

✷✷✷✷✷

Josie hugged her younger sister goodbye.

"I'll get your phone to you," said Caitlyn. "I'll ship it here, but…are you sure you want to stay here?"

"Yeah," breathed Josie. "I think it's better for Houston and I. The Farnsworths said I could stay as long as we want. They've been really kind to us, and they actually want us to stay."

"Okay," shrugged Caitlyn. "I'll let Mom and Dad know, but…you never know…maybe it'll change their minds."

"I doubt it," frowned Josie.

There was nothing more to say about that. That was an old wound, and Josie did not want to reopen it.

Caitlyn gave Houston a kiss on the forehead and then turned toward the entrance of the bus.

Josie took one last look at her sister before the young blonde boarded the bus back home. Caitlyn was a little beat up, but the young woman was tough, and after everything they had both just been through, she was only going to get tougher.

After her sister's sendoff, Josie carried Houston back toward the lot where Henry was waiting with his old red truck.

She walked up to the truck, opened the door, and strapped Houston into his car seat. She got into the truck, picked up the small fishbowl off the floor from between her feet, sat that in her lap, and buckled in.

This fishbowl was important to her, something she had just come into possession of, but it held a value to her beyond words, so she held onto it like a security blanket.

She gave a worried look toward Henry after that, but the old man only smiled at her.

"Don't you worry about a thing," he said gently. "Carol and I know people that will make those boys' vehicles disappear…No one will ever know they were out here…You see? You've got nothing to worry about. You and Houston are safe here."

Josie stared down at the contents of the fishbowl in her lap. That bowl held a flat mound of white sand, and in the middle of that sand was a single stone, Houston's stone, narrow lines spiraling out from the center of that sand to ring around the sides of the glass bowl.

Josie smiled as she stared down at the little stone, because she now had some new protectors in her life, guardians that could make any threats to her or Houston disappear forever.

Yes…they were definitely safe here.

#2…THE BLOOD MARCH

James and the giant breach.

James walked into the bunker behind some young mercs, a bunch of gang-bred newbs all wearing a Red Cobra logo.

These idiots were all packing Bringham-Styles gear, the kind of new crap that wasn't worth its salt on a good day. That was okay for normal enemies, but he seriously doubted anything normal prowled the Blood March. Regular bullets only took you so far, no matter how many you had on you.

The bunker they were all in was really just the remains of a burnt-out building, but the check-in counter was new steel with a set of state-of-the-art rune-tech computers strewn across it. The local commission here must have been subsidized by the federal government, which was good and not good, because though well-funded, the feds were a bunch of incompetent jackhats as far as James was concerned.

"That's two-fifty for minor artifacts, seven hundred for mid-range, and up to three thousand for anything major," he heard the young woman at the check-in counter say.

What a joke. Even a minor artifact could sell for a grand in the hands of someone who knew the right buyer, but James wasn't here for the money. He had something else in mind.

Right now, he was waiting patiently behind this pack of walking bait, but he was being held up, because the lead punk amongst them was currently hitting on the check-in girl.

The young woman behind the counter was cute in the face, a white girl in her very-early twenties with short black hair in a bowl cut, but this annoying gang kid was, of course, interrupting her work by being a complete and total meathead.

"Hey, you should come celebrate with us once we get back," said the lead merc, a kid in his early twenties. "The Red Cobras always need some new blood…You know, you'd look good up on stage, too. They're always looking for new dancers in Brass Port, North Bask. I know a guy at the Swinging Bullet. He'll hook you up."

"Uhhh…" was all the young lady behind the counter could say.

Thankfully, one of the two guards in here, a big bald white guy in his early thirties, this guy decked out in urban-camo-banded-plasti-steel, stepped forward and motioned toward the exit with his Tornham H40 assault rifle.

"Beat it, kid," he growled. "This ain't a daycare. Come back when you hit puberty."

"Hey!" barked the young gang member. "I'm old enough to sign up!"

"It's all right," said the young check-in girl. "They're already in the system."

"Then get your skinny butt out of here," said the bald guard. "You'll get paid if you actually find anything…IF you come out alive."

The band of young mercs laughed at that remark as their punk leader shook his head.

"We're the Red Cobras!" he said in strange excitement. "We ain't afraid of no breachers! They're afraid of us!"

This band of idiots all laughed like their stupidity was the funniest thing in the world.

James wasn't exactly one to throw people to the wolves, but he also didn't stir up unnecessary trouble. Any of these fools that actually did come back out of the labyrinth ahead with all of their limbs still attached? They wouldn't be laughing anymore.

The band of young mercs turned and walked past James, but not before their punk leader opened his mouth one last time, something that always seemed to happen whenever James encountered a group like this.

"Move it, Grandpa," said this young punk.

James completely ignored him. This kid was not worth the trouble of teaching a lesson. A single breacher would do that, and odds were, that lesson would be a permanent one.

James walked around him and up to the counter, and the two guards immediately eyed him with suspicion.

"You're the first pro I've seen all week," said the bald guard. "You look a little old to be doing this, but I'm not stupid. I know a pro when I see one…How'd you get that scar, Mr. Pro?"

James was pushing fifty, flecks of grey starting to show in his short, curly black hair, and no one ever questioned his age, no, but that scar? That scar that ran from right underneath his left eye all the way down to the bottom of his chin? They always asked about that. That scar bedecked his dark skin as a reminder, a reminder to never forget the past or what had been lost in it.

"Got that from grappling a widow's spawn," grunted James. "That was back when I was barely out of my teens."

The young lady at the counter shivered and gave him a wide-eyed, slightly-frightened look.

"Those are real?" she asked.

"Everything's real," replied James.

"Oh…" said the young woman, but she did not question him further on the matter.

No, the big bald guard did that for her.

"How'd you get out of that one?" nodded the guard.

"The place burned to the ground while I was still in it," shrugged James. "Thankfully, those things go up like oil-soaked wicks. I dove out of a second story window and got busted up pretty badly, but I lived."

The other guard, a black man in his late twenties, this man a little younger than the curious bald guard, stepped forward and added his own question to the conversation.

"What about the widow?" he asked.

James shrugged.

"Don't know," he said. "I didn't run into her. She probably burned up like the rest of them."

He had a pretty good idea of what had happened to that overgrown arachnid, but he didn't want to talk about it. That part of his life was long gone. They didn't need to know about his past, and they certainly didn't need to know that he wasn't even from this universe, that he'd crossed over from somewhere else through a breach, a breach much like the one he was about to go raid.

"Huh…" said the bald guard. "What else have you come across?"

James shrugged again.

"A lot," he said.

"Uh, huh," said the bald guard.

James noticed the younger guard eyeing his gun, though he had that relic holstered at the hip.

"Is that a Rune Maker?" asked the younger guard in sudden interest.

James drew his pistol but turned it to the side, resting it across his gloved palms to indicate non-hostility, an important action when dealing with the normal set of trigger-happy guards for these breach sites. He couldn't blame them for being paranoid, though…He knew what came out of these rifts.

"Yeah," he grunted.

The younger guard's eyes went wide as he stepped forward to inspect the well-cared-for six-shooter.

"I didn't think those existed outside of a museum," he breathed.

"Got this twenty years ago," said James matter-of-factly. "It's never let me down."

"I'll bet," replied the guard.

The big bald guard shook his head at his compatriot in arms and then motioned his rifle toward the check-in girl.

"Just sign up here," he said firmly. "I can see that you can take care of yourself, so all you have to do is deliver to us any artifacts you recover. She'll tell you the payrate."

"I heard it," grunted James. "Here's my D-Card."

He holstered his pistol and then unzipped his brown leather belt wallet, removing his identification a moment later.

The young lady at the counter scanned his card and then gave him a friendly smile.

"You're in the system, Mr…uhhh…James," she said. "Is that your first name or your last name?"

"That's my only name," said James.

"Oh," said the young woman in stupid reply. "Well, then, Mr. James, you're all set."

"Good," said James.

He put his ID away and turned to walk out, but his conscience got the better of him. He had to say something about this setup, or it would eat at him later.

He turned and addressed all three of them.

"This isn't a safe place for check-in," he said matter-of-factly. "You're too close to the entrance of the labyrinth."

"We're in a bunker," said the big bald guy. "We're good. Besides, nothing from the breach can cross the Merlin-Crowley line, not without becoming a pile of ash."

"Okay," said James. "I warned you."

"I've got this," said the bald guard as he held up his Tornham H40. "I don't need a warning. It packs a hell of a lot more punch than that museum piece you're wearing."

"Okay," said James.

He knew there were other threats than what could be killed by normal bullets, but it was pointless to tell them that. They weren't going to listen. It was true that no breacher could cross the Merlin-Crowley line— not unless it was really powerful—but the normal human-kind of monster could still take you apart at the knees. Guns would work on them, of course…if you saw them coming.

Still, he didn't like their stubbornness over the matter.

If the two guards wanted to get shredded, that was their business, but he didn't like the thought of this young woman getting killed. He'd seen what could happen at other breach sites, and he doubted the Blood March was any different.

It did not sit well with him, but there was nothing he could do about it. All he could do was finish the job he'd just signed up for, and then when he got back—and he would get back—he'd try and convince that young lady to go find other work, work that didn't involve possibly being sacrificed to an elder god.

He walked out of the bunker and was going to turn left to head toward the entrance of the labyrinth, but he was held up by yet another gang of young punks, though this group was slightly different from the first.

"Oh, you have got to be kidding me," muttered James under his breath.

A group of six young women, all dyed-blondes, all thin, all caked with sparkly makeup, all dressed in matching pink jackets with a butterfly-fairy logo on the backs, came walking up to the bunker entrance.

"Look, ladies," said the lead blonde, a young white woman with a pair of goggles strapped across the top of her dyed-blonde head. "It's senior discount day."

The group of young women laughed as James shook his head no and frowned.

"You got a problem old man?" asked a young Asian woman, her hair also dyed blonde.

James took one look at the assortment of Ailer submachine guns they were strap-carrying and shook his head again. At the very least, a couple of them were carrying grenades, which was definitely a good thing. They were going to need them.

"I'm not that old," he said bluntly. "And this is a combat zone, not a night at the mall."

A young black woman in this group of six, this young woman also with long dyed-blonde hair, scowled at him and addressed the leader of the group.

"Did you hear that, Rene?" she asked. "This old man is insulting us. He says we're going to get mauled."

"That's mall, not ma…" began James. "Never mind."

It was clear they had no idea what a mall was, and there was no way they could possibly know, either.

Their leader scowled as she looked over James with extreme distaste on her makeup-laden face.

"You're looking to get shot," said the lead blonde. "We're the Death Fairies, and you're in our way, so why don't you go die of old age somewhere, Grandpa?"

"Death Fairies, Red Cobras…" muttered James. "It's like the brand names for an energy drink."

"What did you say, old man!" hissed the young black woman. "Say that again!"

"I said 'have fun,'" grunted James. "Keep an eye out for cultists, though."

"Cultists?" asked the young Asian woman. "He thinks we should watch out for cultists?"

The group of young blondes laughed as their leader raised her Ailer SMG and showed it off to James as if it were some kind of educational teaching tool.

"The Ailer 1450 is the most accurate submachine gun on the market," smirked the leader of the group. "I can group a ring of shots at twenty meters within a few millimeters of each other. Those crazies with knives will never get near us."

This young woman stepped forward and stared down at the sword strapped to James' belt, that sword sheathed and hanging from his left hip. Her brown eyes went wide with disgust as she sneered at his selection of weaponry, a clear indication that she had no idea what she was doing.

"You're using that, and you're preaching to me about cultists?" she asked. "Do you see this, girls?...This old man thinks he's going to kill a breacher with this overgrown pigsticker!"

The young women laughed and surrounded him like a pack of hyenas.

He didn't bother to tell them that this "overgrown pigsticker" was a genuine 1860 Union Cavalry Saber that he'd taken with him when he'd crossed over to this realm. He didn't bother to tell them that he'd had it etched with twelve different runes, something that had cost him a small fortune to do, and he certainly didn't bother to tell them that it had saved his life more than once. Such an explanation would have been wasted on them.

The young Asian woman stepped forward and pointed a finger in his face.

"Don't lecture us about cultists, Grandpa!" she barked.

James shook his head. This was pointless. He probably wasn't going to see these girls again, at least not alive anyway, but he felt obligated to warn them anyhow.

"They won't eat you like a breacher," he said matter-of-factly. "No, a breacher will eat you, maybe lay eggs in you, but cultists?...They just kill and dismember the men, but they like to strip young women like yourself and sacrifice them through ritual torture. I've seen it more than once."

These young ladies all laughed in his face, but he was used to this kind of reaction. No one ever listened to him anyway.

"Whatever, Grandpa," said the young Asian woman. "Any of those nutjobs tries to gank me, I'm going to take his knife and cut off his—"

"Don't waste your breath on this dinosaur," smirked the leader of the group. "Come on, girls. Let's go make some easy money...I want a new pair of boots."

They laughed again as they pushed past him, but James let them go unhindered. He wanted to smack them around just like he'd wanted to smack around the previous group, talk some sense into them, but that wasn't going to happen. He already knew they wouldn't listen. He'd seen enough horror to last three lifetimes, but there was one inevitable truth that never changed...No one ever listened.

James continued on his way to the entrance of the labyrinth. That entrance lay between two huge walls of fallen concrete, the cracked and broken pavement beneath it marked with protective runes laced in etched gold.

The various runes upon the ground glowed with a white, slightly-blue light as he approached them, and then he crossed past that threshold, past the Merlin-Crowley line, feeling the slight burn and buzz from that barrier as he walked into the labyrinth proper of the Blood March.

Time worked differently in a breach zone; hours and minutes were warped, unstable. There was no telling how many creatures had actually come out of the breach, so things were about to get…interesting.

He reached up and pressed in the button on his steel neck collar. He did have some state-of-the-art tech on him because he wasn't stupid, but only the useful ones, and his Hermes-Alliette retractable helm was one of these useful devices. Not only did it protect his head, but it came with a full heads-up-display with advanced spectral sighting.

The banded helm raised from the inside of his collar, completely covering his head and face, a corrugated breathing mask across his mouth, his eyes covered by a pair of amber visors. If he were going to die today, it wasn't going to be from a headshot or toxic gas.

"Warning," came a polite female voice through his helmet.

James tapped his helmet once. His combat VI was working, and that was good. It had been on the fritz ever since he'd been knocked through a wall by a charging minotaur, but his personal tech, Lazarus Radditz, had fixed it for him, though that repair had not been cheap.

"Warning," came the voice of his VI again. "Multiple-Class Lovecraftians in area. Advise caution."

"Yep," grunted James.

He drew his Rune Maker and walked down the deserted street.

There were abandoned burnt-out buildings of concrete and shattered glass on both sides of him, the air around him thick with an aura of ominous portent. This was a good place to get ambushed, but it was far enough away from the breach that it was probably only a Class-One Threat Zone.

Nevertheless, he was cautious if anything…That trait had kept him alive longer than anything else.

Whenever a breach opened, it would scatter items from other universes along a conical path, and these "artifacts," no matter how mundane-looking, were always endowed with dimensional energy, making them worth their weight in gold. That's why the State wanted them, but James wasn't interested in what the State wanted, nor had he ever been.

No, the best selection was always right next to the breach, and unfortunately, that was where the worst of the cosmos lurked as well, so the danger increased the nearer one got to one of these accursed openings.

He heard shouts and gunfire in the distance, off to his left. Naturally, he turned right.

Breach Rule #1: Never go where there's gunfire.

Other mercs were opening up on whatever, but James knew better than to head in that direction. Those other mercs were either handling the situation, or they were getting torn to pieces, and either way, his goal was to find artifacts, not get caught up in some needless firefight.

It seemed a little cold and heartless when he thought about it, but this was the way you survived when inside a breach zone. You didn't screw around, you didn't touch anything that looked suspicious, and you didn't, absolutely did not, waste bullets for someone else.

Yeah, that meant he was alone ninety-percent of the time, but he'd survived this long on his own, and he trusted his own judgement far more than he trusted anyone else's. He'd been a fool in the past, and that foolishness had nearly gotten him killed more than once…Never again.

He took a side street as he pulled a pocket watch from one of his brown leather jacket's inner pockets. He flipped open the watch and stared down at the needles, the short hand pointing toward nine while the long hand pointed toward halfway between three and four. The seconds hand didn't move at all, mainly because it didn't do anything.

His watch didn't tell time. No, this little artifact pointed toward the nearest open breach with its hours hand and toward the barrier line with its minutes hand. It was a useful little device he'd picked up early on, and it was proving more than useful now.

"Warning," stated his VI. "Class-One Lovecraftians in area."

"Yeah, yeah," said James in return.

He closed his pocket watch, put it back in his interior pocket, and traveled down this side street, though he knew he was going to have to turn left at some point.

He spied a body in the distance, and he gripped his gun in ready wariness as he walked up to it.

There was a dead male in the street, six feet stretched out if the head were still attached, but the head was missing.

Considering where he'd come from, he switched between meters and feet all the time. This universe used the metric system for some reason, but James was old-school American, so he still used the English system, so over time, he'd learned to use both.

Whatever the case, he needed to inspect this body.

This body was dressed in ripped black jeans and an open, punk-studded, black leather jacket, black leather boots on his feet. In his right hand was an older-model Jacobs-Brill light SMG, model 739, the finger still on the trigger. There was a large bloody hole in the jeans right above the crotch, a stab wound, but that could mean anything.

"Head missing, large puncture wound in upper groin…" breathed James. "Not enough info."

It would have been nice if he'd had more information to work with.

"Warning," stated his helmet VI. "Class-One Lovecraftians in area."

"I got that," muttered James.

He briefly took that opportunity to look around the street for obvious threats, looking up as well, because you could never be too careful.

"Warning," stated his VI. "Class-One Lovecraftians in area."

"I said, I got tha—" he began, but he didn't finish that statement.

It was the bubbling up of flesh inside the corpse that made him back off, the sudden change making him back away from this lone body in the street.

The bare stomach of the body bulged as multiple round shapes pushed up against that dead flesh.

"Son of a…" began James.

He reached down and placed his gloved left hand over the flame rune on his bulletproof vest. He did this out of both instinct and experience, because he knew what he was dealing with now.

The rune on his vest glowed a bright-red as an orange barrier popped up around him. The barrier covered him like an egg patterned out with hexagonal etches, spanning out from him a few decimeters, giving him just enough room to move without getting scorched.

The bubbled flesh of the corpse tore outwards as a swarm of mouths with insectile wings burst out of the body and made a beeline for him.

"Warning," stated his VI. "Class-One Lovecraftians in area."

"I know!" yelled James.

A small cloud of flying red mouths, each with distinctly human teeth and tiny human-like legs below those human-sized lips, swarmed around him, but they couldn't get past his hastily erected barrier. They burst into flames as they made contact with it, burning up like bugs that had made contact with a bug zapper for too long.

This emergency flame barrier of his was for just this purpose, but it wouldn't last long. The portable magical charge held in the rune on his vest could only keep up the barrier for less than a minute, and then it would have to recharge, but those precious few seconds it was active was usually enough to deal with a swarm…usually.

These things were fairly large, each about the size of a rat, but there weren't many of them. Only problem was, they were persistent, burning away to ash as they tried to chew through the orange barrier around him, and that barrier was giving out.

"Screw it," said James.

He used his left-hand to switch off the barrier, simultaneously aiming at the last of the nasty little things attempting to get at him.

He fired a regular bullet from his Rune Maker, not bothering to switch to a magical charge. He was using .45 ammo, so one half of this red mouth with wings blew apart as the other half dropped to the ground.

One last one he had not noticed attached itself to his helmet, but James quickly grabbed it with his left hand, tossed it to the ground, and stomped on it repeatedly with his left boot. He had on good leather boots that would last awhile, and the soles were fairly tough, so he had no reservations about squishing this thing into paste.

"Nasty…little…piece…of…" he growled as he stomped it into liquid jelly, stomping on it with each breath of word.

"Warning," stated his helmet VI. "Class-Two Lovecraftian in area."

He snapped his attention toward farther down the street, and that's when the next threat rounded the corner of a burnt-out building from a connecting street.

It was big, at least eight-feet-tall, of skinny build, the serrated chitin of an insect covering its warped, disgusting body. Its head was a giant human mouth with broad, flat, white teeth, each tooth the size of a playing card, the lips big red things that spread across at least a full meter. It stood upon two bow-legged, blood-colored, human legs, legs with the thick muscle of a weight lifter in stark contrast to its stick build. Its arms were of the same make, two big pro-wrestler looking arms that were each as thick around as James' neck.

"Yep," said James. "There it is."

This thing had a giant arrowhead abdomen hanging down between its legs, a huge black stinger pointing downwards from that abdomen. Most disturbing, however, was the soft peach-colored skin of its belly, that belly displaying a human male head with its eyes closed, that head's mouth open as if it were trying to moan in pain.

"Ymir's Breath," said James quickly.

An etched rune on the barrel of his Rune Maker lit up with a bright-blue light upon receiving the incantation necessary to activate it.

This thing, this cosmic horror from somewhere outside the reaches of sanity, opened up its huge maw and roared. The sound reverberated down the street, echoing off the cracked and broken concrete walls, and this would have popped the eardrums of any normal person hearing it, but James' VI automatically muted his outside hearing upon receiving this attack, something he was suddenly infinitely grateful for.

Just one of these things would have driven a normal person insane upon seeing and hearing it, but James was far too hardened for that to work on him.

"You can't shake me, big lips," he said firmly. "I've been to Missouri."

It charged on those two bowed and muscular legs, its big-lipped head bobbing up and down upon its skinny neck, and though it was far faster than it appeared to be, it did not make it to him.

James fired off four rounds in succession, striking the beast center mass, and it slowed down with each shot as frost crawled out from the bullet wounds, coating it over with a thin layer of blue ice, coating it over until the creature was frozen in place, white hoarfrost covering it from its big-lipped head to its big bare toes.

James only had one bullet left in the chamber, but one bullet was all he needed.

"Banshee's Wail," he said firmly.

A rune on the barrel of his gun lit up in bright neon purple as he aimed his piece, and then he pulled the trigger, feeling that familiar kick of recoil once more.

The bullet struck center mass, leaving a small hole in the frozen flesh of this thing. There was a high-pitched whine a second later, and then a visible ripple in the air blew outwards in a half-sphere of sonic destruction from the center of the frosty statue, the frozen beast shattering into so many icy chunks that there was essentially nothing left of it.

"Iced," said James.

He took the time to reload his Rune Maker with regular .45 rounds. Guns anymore used enchanted ammo, the runes already embedded in the bullet casings, a much cheaper and more efficient way to carry around any necessary destruction, but James preferred his Rune Maker, dinosaur that it was. His relic enchanted bullets as they were fired, and this allowed him to cover any situation. His piece had variability and class, two things these young merc punks had lost in the filing.

Of course, etched on his pistol weren't actual Norse runes. They were glyphs or sigils or some such crap…Ritual circles?…. He had no idea what they were; he only knew that they worked, and that was all that mattered. Everyone in this world called them "runes," so…whatever.

James holstered his piece, pulled out his pocket watch, and checked his location. He needed to go west, so heading down the street where the big-lipped creature had come from was his only current option.

He put away his watch, headed down the street, and made a left onto the appropriate street. He was going in the right direction, but considering he was at a breach site, that didn't mean much. He was going to get jumped no matter what direction he took.

There was nothing around him but burnt-out buildings and trash, nothing that could possibly have any rift energy attached to it. Besides, he'd know an artifact when he saw one. Inexperienced mercs might not know, but he would. He'd been to way too many of these places, and the Blood March was no different.

"Rift-energy signature detected," stated his VI.

He did not get far before he spied something bright and colorful off to his right, something in the rubble next to a hollowed-out, burnt-out car, the make and model of the vehicle long unidentifiable.

He walked up to the rubble and pulled forth a small, neatly-wrapped present about the size of his hand, the paper over it in red-and-white-striped Christmas colors, a ragged green bow atop it. This was a rare find, something intact that had been flung out this far when the breach in question had exploded into existence.

He tore open the paper and revealed a small, black, cardboard box. He carefully opened it to inspect what was inside, and James was pleasantly surprised at what he'd found.

Inside the small giftbox was a silver chain necklace with a little, flat, silver heart attached to it. He seriously doubted the chain was made from real silver, but that was beside the point. This little necklace was intact, and it had clearly come from the rift, so it was imbued with eldritch energy, and that made it extremely valuable.

He could see the aura of power emanating from this necklace through his helmet feed. The silver chain and box both glowed with an orange light, the numbers in his HUD revealing that this little lost present was well within the rare range, a great find to just up and stumble across.

What the chain and box actually did power-wise, he did not know, but that was not his problem. Someone else could deal with that.

But he was not here for that. No, there were better finds than this, and he was going to find them; that was a guarantee.

He closed the box and stuffed the whole thing into his interior right jacket pocket. He'd added a number of pockets to this jacket, a necessity while out in the field, and his pockets had the Deep enchantment, making them able to hold more than they possibly could otherwise.

"Well, that's some pocket money," he muttered.

He took out his pocket watch and checked his direction. Why his watch held a compass power instead of a temporal one, he had no idea, but rift magic didn't follow anyone's rules, so when something was imbued with a power, that was the power it held, period. It was true that some items could always be depended upon for a particular power, but pocket watches were not one of those items.

He shook his head clear of thoughts and studied his watch. He was headed due west, exactly where he needed to go.

He hit a four-way, no stop signs, the remains of traffic lights up and still strung across the way, something from the past, a distant memory, but he was long over that life.

The stench here would have been unbearable if not for his helmet, but that caustic odor was due to the sheer number of corpses everywhere. He could actually see that film of rotting stench in his HUD, kind of like wisps of black smoke rising from the bodies in the four-way.

"What the…?" he asked himself.

Around him were the previous remains of other mercs, some of them so rotted that they had to have been here for quite some time. There were logos or gang signs or whatever you wanted to call them on various bits of clothing here and there, male and female bodies, some stripped, some partially eaten, all dead.

"Warning," stated his VI. "Class-One Corporeal Undead in area."

"Ugh…" breathed James. "Zombies."

Zombies were the low end of the undead. He'd run into their kind many a time in the past, but he had a solution for them that had never let him down.

"Ifrit's Rage," he spoke, and a rune on the barrel of his gun glowed with a bright-orange light.

Breach Rule #2: Never enter an area filled with bodies.

He was going to break this rule, however. He needed to head west, and this four-way was the only path west without going through a building, and going through a building was actually more dangerous than breaking one of his own rules. Besides, he could deal with zombies.

Breach Rule #3: Never enter a building if there's another less-dangerous way.

He stepped into the midst of the four-way, into the midst of moldering bodies around him, and this was a tactical mistake, true, but not a serious one.

The problem with corpses strung out like this was that you never knew which ones were still active, like stepping into a partially-cleared minefield, so you could get surrounded fairly quickly, and with zombies, numbers were what mattered. Too many could overwhelm you, but that was also the reason he carried an enchanted sword, because that blade was useful in a pinch and had been many times before.

His attention turned to something more important, however, because he saw some mercs up ahead, some standing gang members from the Red Cobras, though there were only two in his field of vision.

"Warning," stated his helmet VI. "Class-One Corporeal Undead in area."

One of the mercs turned around, and James recognized the leader of these young punks, or rather, what was left of him. Half of the young man's face was gone, the right half, his teeth showing where his lips had once been, a bloody smear of muscle on chunked flesh where his face should have connected at the nose.

The leader staggered toward him, arms raised, but the dead young man was a good seven meters away, nothing to worry about.

James raised his pistol and waited for the leader to close in, waiting until the walking deceased was within the four-meter range before pulling the trigger of his gun. His Rune Maker fired with a loud bang, and that enchanted bullet went right through the punk leader's good eye, setting the mobile corpse's head aflame with that single shot.

"Ashes to ashes…" said James.

The leader fell burning to the street to join the other bodies, but he was burned to ash within seconds of active incineration.

The sound of the shot had attracted the attention of the remaining merc of the Red Cobras, and he turned around to stagger toward James, but James put him down as easily as the first. This wasn't even a mercy killing, no, as they were only corpses animated by dark magic, their souls long gone. This was simply cremation.

"Dust to dust," finished James.

"Warning," stated his helmet VI. "Class-One Corporeal Undead in area."

Bodies around him twitched and started to stand, immediately provoking James into a fight or flight response.

"Tricky sons of…" he started, but he had more immediate concerns than finishing that expletive.

He fired around him, ashing four of them before they could fully stand, but his pistol was empty after that, and there was no time to reload.

He quickly holstered his Rune Maker and drew his saber, ready to cut his way out.

"Seraph's Light," he stated, and a rune on the long blade in his right hand blazed with a white light.

A pair of walking dead came at him from his peripheral right, but he beheaded the first one with a single slice of his blade, the head popping off as the body burst with holes of light from the magic flowing through it, the enchanted strike disintegrating the corpse with ease.

James cut the right arm off the other one, and it, too, disintegrated before it even hit the ground.

He was surrounded after that by six of them, all of them staggering toward him, arms raised, rotted fingers out, the hungry dead ready to tear him apart. James sliced around himself in a practiced sword dance, something he'd learned through sheer experience, and then they were no more, those shuffling bodies gone, disintegrated by holy magic.

James sheathed his sword and shook his head. It was likely the previous band of mercs, the Red Cobras, had been ambushed in the stupidest way possible, but that was not his problem. They had walked straight into this four-way, but unlike him, they had not known what they were dealing with.

It didn't matter. Judging by the bullet holes in some of these corpses, the Red Cobras had done him a favor anyway. They had cleared out most of this little army of undead.

He walked forward toward the two piles of ash that were the remains of the two Cobras he'd put down.

"Nothing left," he muttered.

There was no gear to salvage, not that he needed their stuff anyway. He was more interested in why there was a minefield of zombies here at a four-way.

He spied it after that, a necromantic circle drawn directly at the center of this four-way, or rather, chipped into the asphalt. The circle was covered in intricately drawn symbols, and it only took human blood to activate that dark magic. Blood was about the cheapest resource in a breach area, and this particular breach was titled "The Blood March," after all.

A young woman flickered into view within the circle. She was completely nude, blonde, tied to a wooden pole, big breasted, beautiful face, an hourglass figure, something most mercs would rush to rescue right away, especially those Red Cobra idiots.

"Help me!" cried the young woman. "Somebody, help me!"

James shook his head at this low-tier obvious illusion. It was a lure like any other, like peanut butter in a mouse trap. Mercs wandered in, the dead rose around them, end of story.

This was a problem. Anyone that died here would invariably come back as a zombie.

He could destroy the symbol animating them, but it was etched into the street, and true, he could take out that symbol with one Banshee round, but firing at it would just cause the bullet to ricochet.

Yes, his rounds could be enchanted due to his Rune Maker, but they were still physical bullets, after all, and bullets still followed the laws of physics unless "told" otherwise. His rounds actually had to lodge in something in order to activate anyway.

James took to reloading his pistol, shaking his head in frustration. He had to find some way to close the breach or, at least, notify someone of this necro-four-way. He didn't think much of other mercs in general, but this was a trap, and traps were primarily a human weapon. That meant a necromancer, which was bad, or cultists, which was also bad, though both were bad in different ways.

He couldn't narrow down the culprit just yet. Both necromancers and cultists could create zombies, but they summoned different things, and all of those things were terrible.

Necromancers were solitary but deadly, so fighting one of them was going to be tough. On the other hand, cultists traveled in packs, but they were easier to take out. However, the things cultists summoned were objectively worse than anything a necromancer could conjure up, so in essence…both were equally bad.

"There were Lovecraftians in the area," muttered James. "That's usually cultists, but the breach could have spit out the Lovecrafts…Hmmm…Don't know yet."

He pulled out his pocket watch, checked his direction, put his watch away, and took toward the west street. It was time to get moving anyway.

There was a dozen dead mercs on this new street, some ripped apart, some partially eaten, but all dead. Whatever had killed them had moved on, and that something was big, but that was not his problem. This new, unknown breacher was probably a Class Three, maybe even a Class Four, so his only problem was avoiding it altogether. Whatever the case, these mercs hadn't stood a chance.

He ignored them and continued on in the direction his watch had indicated; his original mission was to find artifacts, after all.

He felt so much as saw himself pass through some sort of energy barrier. It was a tingling of sorts, a crackle in the air, and this set him on edge.

"That can't be good," muttered James.

"Warning," stated his VI. "Class-Five Disparate Entity in area."

"That is definitely not good," said James quietly.

The breach was most certainly in this location, too. This…complicated things.

For one thing, his helmet VI was no longer going to inform him of any rift energy in the area, because this area was all rift energy. That meant he had to manually locate artifacts. However, it turned out that locating anything of value was not going to be a problem.

He walked toward the end of the street, that street littered with knickknacks here and there, some broken, some intact, and he picked up what he could. He snatched up a snow globe, a deck of playing cards, and a first-aid kit, of all things.

The snow globe could have any power…He wasn't sure. The playing cards, however, were dangerous. There was no telling what each individual card did, and each one had a one-time use, so…he'd be selling that right away. Some other sucker could test it. The first-aid kit, though?…Now that was valuable…if it still had anything in it.

He quickly opened the white plastic box and realized it was mostly full.

"Jackpot," he said firmly. "It's payday, but I'm not done yet."

Most of what came out of a breach was trash, but sometimes…sometimes you got lucky, and this was one of those times.

But his attention was taken by something else.

He could clearly see the breach now. It was pretty big, about twelve-feet-tall and eight-feet-wide, a glowing portal of blue and white light, definitely large enough for a Class-Five otherworlder to pass through.

"Warning," stated his helmet VI. "Class-Five Disparate Entity in area."

"Yeah," stated James in return.

He gripped the pistol of his Rune Maker and visually scanned the area for threats, but he did not have to scan for long.

"Mortal," came a deep and echoing voice from behind him.

James swiveled and leveled his pistol at this new threat.

The man standing before him was tall, of Arabic descent, and dressed in a grey three-piece suit. This new guy sported fine, slicked-back, black hair and slimline shades upon the hawkish nose of his sharp and unforgiving face, and his demeanor was cold and rigid, like a living statue without an emotion to spare.

James could feel the power radiating off of this guy, and his HUD was going crazy with energy readings, but the stranger hadn't attacked, so James knew something was up, and that something was never good.

"What is it you desire, mortal?" asked the stranger.

"Warning," stated James' VI. "Class-Five Disparate Entity in area."

"Raijin's Thunder," spoke James.

The appropriate rune on his piece lit up with a bright yellow light, and the stranger backed away a couple of feet.

"You are to leave this place," said James firmly.

"Is that what you desire?" asked the man.

James knew what he was dealing with now, but this particular threat required…negotiation…along with a healthy dose of intimidation.

"I don't make deals with Djinn," said James.

"All mortals desire something," replied the man, this "Djinn."

"Maybe…" stated James. "But I know better than to wish for anything around one of your kind."

"You may have anything you wish for," said the Djinn.

"Warning," stated James' helmet VI. "Class-Five Disparate…"

"Protocol Alpha," stated James. "Disregard Class-Five Disparate-Entity warnings."

"Noted," stated his VI. "Disregarding Class-Five Disparate-Entity warnings."

He'd have to reset that later, but he had a more immediate problem right in front of him.

"Tell me your desire, mortal," said the Djinn. "You have done well to reach me."

James held up his pistol and pulled back the hammer.

"I'm not like the others," he said firmly. "I'm letting you live, but only because I need this breach closed…There's no wish from me. You will pull one thing from your 'pockets' that I want, and then you will walk right through that breach and close it behind you."

"You cannot threaten me, mortal," warned the Djinn. "Something must be offered…It cannot be taken."

But James knew better. He'd dealt with a Djinn before, and he knew exactly what they were like.

"You're without your fetter," said James. "That's why you wandered through the breach. You have to be granted a new one, or you're stuck here at half power. That's why you're feeding off of others…You're going to fade without a permanent home, and you know most of these idiots around here can't make it to you…You won't find any food stuck here. You're going to starve."

James pulled out the snow globe from one of his many jacket pockets and held it up.

"This is rift-charged," he said. "That means it's unbreakable…so we'll make a trade, your new fetter for my terms. I won't make a wish, but I'll trade."

The Djinn lowered his head as if thinking, and then he raised his shaded gaze to stare back at James, a slight smile on his sharp face.

"That is acceptable," nodded the Djinn. "State what it is you wish to trade for."

"I don't wish for anything," snorted James, "but I know what I want, and so do you. You already know what I want, and I know better than to say it out loud. Give it to me, then get in the globe. I'll throw it through the breach. You can end up somewhere else, just not here. Close the breach behind you after that…That's the trade…There's no wish, and you know that, so make a trade or don't waste my time."

The man, this "Djinn," took off his slimline shades and stared at James with soulless and pupilless blood-red eyes. He frowned, his lips turning downwards in noted displeasure, but James knew he would capitulate.

Breach Rule #…Whatever: Don't ever give a Djinn a choice, and don't ever…*ever*…wish for anything around them.

"It is a trade, then" nodded the Djinn.

The Djinn reached into his suit pocket and pulled forth what James had been searching for for many years now. James quickly took it, placed that highly-prized object into one of his interior-jacket pockets, and held up the snow globe in his gloved left hand.

The Djinn transformed into a cloud of grey smoke, and then that grey smoke was sucked into the snow globe in James' waiting left hand. That small cloud swirled around inside the globe, fake snow in the liquid whirling around with it, the little buildings inside completely obscured from view.

James turned and hucked the globe through the breach, and then there was a burst of energy from the opening that knocked him backwards, but he caught himself before he could fall.

The portal spit out an array of blue-lightning that crackled across it, and then it collapsed in on itself, disappearing without a trace.

"Done and done," muttered James. "Now to get out of this hellhole."

The breach was closed, but whatever had come through it wasn't gone. Breachers had to be "manually" removed, but that was not his problem. No, he had what he needed here, more than he needed, in fact, much more, so it was time for him to leave.

"Let's blow this pop stand," he said firmly.

He kept his pistol ready as he made his way east. Couldn't be too careful.

He made his way back to the four-way and took a moment to study the ritual circle etched into the center of that intersection. He would have to notify someone about that later. It was simply too dangerous to leave here. Of course, any zombies here were already destroyed, so…a cleanup crew could safely deal with it in case he couldn't contact anyone.

His mental waffling over the matter only made him shake his head. He needed to get back with his remaining goods, and this was just a distraction.

He made a mental decision at that moment…It was a shorter route to just take the south street rather than doubling back from whence he'd come. Any breachers would be scrambling for the exit to the Blood March, but just because the breach was closed did not mean the Merlin-Crowley line was down. Any breachers hitting that would be ashed almost instantly.

There was, of course, whatever had killed those mercs right before reaching the breach, and he wanted to avoid that unknown at all costs. Hopefully, whatever had raged through that street had been ashed at the Merlin-Crowley line by now.

He made his way down this southern street when he came across what was left of the Death Fairies. There were several bodies here, most of them missing limbs, one missing her head. There was a leg off to his right and a female body ripped in half to his left, but his attention was on the corpse of a giant wolf lying in the center of the street.

It was impressive that they had been able to take that thing down, because he was pretty sure this dead wolf was a shadow beast, rift-charged and ready for slaughter, at least a Class-Three.

It had probably been a dire wolf, but going through the breach had supercharged it, making it even bigger and faster than it should have been, because it was as big as a Clydesdale, bigger, in fact. Taking it down with just regular firearms was an actual feat, something the mercs in front of the breach had not been able to do…It had been the Death Fairies first and final accomplishment.

"Solves that mystery," grunted James.

But he heard movement off to his right.

James saw her a second later, the young black woman sitting on the sidewalk, her back against a burnt-out building, her dyed-blonde hair stained with sprayed blood. The young woman was missing her right arm, but more than that…She was holding an arm with her left hand, and she was trying to reattach that arm to her bloody stump.

She looked up as James approached her, her dark eyes wide and wild.

"It won't fit," she said, her voice thick with shock. "I can't get it to fit…I keep trying, but it won't fit."

The arm she was trying to attach had clearly belonged to a white girl, so it wasn't even her arm.

"You're in shock," said James matter-of-factly. "That's not even your arm."

The young woman stared down at the arm in her possession and blinked at it as if seeing it for the first time.

"Oh…" she said quietly.

She dropped the arm to the sidewalk and stared at the bloody stump where her right arm had been.

James was sometimes callous, and he knew that—tragedy had hardened him a number of ways—but he wasn't heartless.

He pulled forth his first-aid kit, the one he'd found near the breach, and popped it open. There was no reason to let this poor kid bleed out. He'd had that kit attached to his belt via a leather loop, and he hadn't planned on using it unless there was an emergency, but he figured this qualified.

He pulled forth a bandage packet and ripped open the paper, pulling out the bandage for ready use. This girl was fortunate that he had found this artifact, because if he hadn't, she was going to join her friends shortly.

"Here," he said as he knelt down next to her.

"They all died except for me and Chie," said the young black woman. "It bit off Rene's head, and Chie ran. The others shot it, and…and I shot it…but it killed everyone. They're all dead…"

"You're in shock," said James. "This is going to hurt, and I don't have anything for you to bite down on, so you're going to have to scream. You don't want to bite down on your tongue."

This young woman stared at him with uncomprehending eyes.

"O…kay…" she drawled out.

He could tell she was fading, so there was no time to dawdle.

He placed the bandage over the bleeding stump. A light flared up from the one-use artifact, a blinding-white light, and the young woman screamed, a shrill and terrible thing to hear at close range, but James had been expecting it.

The light died a few seconds later, dying out as this young woman's scream died down at the same time, and James removed the bloody, spent bandage from the wound.

The stump had healed over with new skin, an instantaneous healing, the reason James had wanted to keep everything in the kit intact, but he didn't regret using the bandage. It had served its intended purpose.

"It…It doesn't hurt anymore," said the young black woman.

"Come on," said James.

He pulled her up by her remaining arm, but she had trouble standing. She limped along as James helped her via his arm around her waist, her left arm around his shoulders.

"You're that old guy," said the young woman.

"I'm not that old," said James. "Getting there, but not yet…What's your name, kid?"

"Sofie," said the young woman.

"Come on, Sofie," said James. "Let's get you out of here. Let's both get out of here."

"Yeah…" said Sofie.

"You said one of your friends ran off?" asked James.

"Yeah," said Sofie. "Chie ran."

"She might still be alive then," said James.

They turned left and walked down an eastern street, but James' helmet VI had issued no warnings, so everything was good for the moment.

They made it close to the entrance to the Blood March, close to the Merlin-Crowley line, before they spotted her.

The young Asian woman, the one named Chie, hadn't made it.

Her nude body was laid out in a ritual circle, the heart removed, the more sensitive parts of her body cut off, taken for God knew what purpose, and on her face was a look of pure agony and terror, her eyes squeezed shut, her mouth wide open from screaming, that open orifice filled with her own blood.

Sofie choked once upon seeing her dead friend, and then she sobbed as she broke down completely, her shock finally ending with that grisly sight.

"Don't look," said James. "Just turn away."

She sobbed as she bound her gaze, closing her eyes as she nodded in poignant acceptance of his advice.

It was better this way. This young woman, Sofie, didn't need to be doing this, not the kind of merc-work James was used to.

But he had a bigger problem. It was clear there was a cultist infestation going on, and he knew that now, so unless those two yahoos guarding the entry point had killed those crazies—which he highly frickin' doubted—then he wasn't getting paid by them.

Still, he had something better than money, so the money wasn't really all that big of a deal, but that didn't solve the cultist problem. Those nutjobs were just going to reopen the breach if they weren't dealt with here and now.

James and his new charge crossed the Merlin-Crowley line, and they spotted the bodies right after that.

Ambushed…It's what cultists do.

Both guards were dead, their limbs and heads cut off, their naked torsos piked upon makeshift poles, their heads on separate poles, their limbs in a nearby pile. There was a bloody line of twine tied between the two main poles, that twine holding their severed fingers, toes, and…other parts.

This grisly display was typical cultist work when dealing with men, not a ritual, just an intimidation tactic to keep anyone from closing the breach.

Sofie sobbed once in audible horror at the sight, but James shushed her.

"You stay put," said James. "There are cultists here…I know where these crazies are, and I'll deal with them. Once it's safe, I'll come and get you."

"Don't leave me!" whispered the young woman.

"You'll be fine," he said firmly. "You just wait here…I have to go step on some bugs."

But James had to forcefully sit her down. She struggled a bit, but she was weak from blood loss, so she capitulated without further argument. Besides, he knew what to do.

"Just cover your eyes," he said. "I'll be back shortly. You may hear some screaming, but it won't be me."

Of that, he was certain.

She covered her face with her only remaining hand and wept into it. He felt a twinge of sympathy for her, but he'd be back to get her after he'd cleared out an infestation, so this was only wasting his time. He needed that time to rescue the young receptionist that had checked him in, or at least, confirm that she was already dead.

He took his leave of the last Death Fairie after that, this time making his way toward the entrance of the check-in bunker.

"They'll take time to draw out the circle," muttered James. "They have to strip her, bind her, get things ready…"

He knew how these crazies worked. Once they'd cleared out any guards, they would start their ritual, and once that was started, they were vulnerable.

James drew his saber as he stepped into the bunker.

On the floor was the receptionist, completely stripped of her clothing, tied down in a ritual circle, but she was still alive for the moment, uninjured, though that would not last long. It was a good thing he'd shown up now, because she only had seconds before the torture was to begin.

There were six of them, all in dirty brown robes, their faces covered with boils, their hands in bloody white rags, their eyes wild with whatever eldritch insanity had possessed them.

Their leader held a wicked-looking curved dagger in his right hand, and he slowly lowered the murderous weapon toward the young receptionist, the point aimed directly at her bare breasts, that sharp blade meant for flaying sensitive skin, that flaying to be played out in a slow, deliberate manner. It was no surprise that her dark eyes were wide with panic and terror, an appropriate response for the situation at hand.

"P…Please!" she whined. "Don't do this! Please! I'll give you anything you want!"

James was upon them before they could turn or even notice him. He stabbed the nearest cultist through the back to where his blade exited the chest, that cultist's blood spraying in an arc all over the bare flesh of the receptionist about to be tortured to death.

He withdrew his blade by planting one leather boot into the back of the cultist he had just stabbed, kicking off the body with practiced ease, and he sliced through the neck of the next cultist before that one could retaliate, the scumbag's diseased head popping free to spray up blood in a red fountain from the remaining neck stump.

James didn't need any magic for this…These walking filth could be taken care of the good old-fashioned way.

The remaining four were on him after that, knives drawn, ready to slice and dice.

Warning reticles popped up in his HUD from various angles, and he mentally tracked them as those threats zoomed toward him in slow time.

A blade sliced down in an arc from his peripheral left, but James cut free that hand before the weapon could ever reach him, and that filth-ridden bandaged hand flew across the enclosed bunker area, still gripping a curved dagger meant solely for murder.

James punched the next cultist in the face before the raving maniac could react, a staggering left jab that gave him enough time to run the man through.

He shoved off the body with a shoulder ram, withdrawing his bloody saber with that action, and he spun in a circle, beheading the stunned handless cultist with that whirling swing. He spun again to smash the hilt of his sword into the nose of the third one, cutting down across the right knee after that, then slicing once more to remove the head once that cultist had dropped to his injured right knee.

There was blood everywhere now, blood spraying from headless neck stumps and leaking from stab wounds, but this was "The Blood March" after all, so it was earning that title, and in the worst way.

There was only the leader left now, the leader of this pile of dung that had betrayed humanity, and all of this bloody nonsense was a breaking point for James, something that had finally and truly angered him.

"Ifrit's Rage," stated James, and the flame rune on his saber lit up with an orange light.

No, he didn't need magic for this scum-sucking piece of filth, but he was angry now, so all bets were off.

The leader stepped forward, curved dagger raised, but this was a ruse. This boil-ridden, disgusting betrayer parted his crusted lips as if to scream, but a black snake shot from his open mouth, the venomous serpent shooting forward straight toward James' helmeted face.

"Warning," stated his helmet VI. "Hostile—"

James completely ignored his VI as he swung his saber up and in an arc to slice the serpent in twain, the snake erupting in flames as it was severed into two parts, that deadly magical flame spreading down the bodyline of the serpent to enter the mouth of the cultist leader, and then the fanatic's head burst into flames from the inside out, his eyes popping like grapes in a microwave, no screams from him as James planted one boot in his chest to kick him back and over.

"Die in obscurity," spat James.

He flicked dark blood from his saber, pulled an old rag from one of his many pockets, and wiped his blade clean. He tossed the rag away, shook his head once, and sheathed his sword.

He was going to have to get another rag. Cultists were about as unclean as you got.

James undid the receptionist's bonds after that, and the young woman scrambled to find what was left of her clothes, though those were pretty much rags at this point. Even so, she clutched those rags to herself, hiding her naked parts as best she could, but James didn't care about that. He needed to finish this business here and now.

"Breach is closed," he said firmly. "You need to get out of here."

"Wh…What?" asked the young woman.

"Breach is closed," he stated again. "I closed it…The Blood March is done."

"Oh…" said the young woman.

He nodded toward the entrance of the bunker.

"What's your name?" he asked.

"B…Brenda," stammered the young woman.

"I've got an injured merc outside, Brenda," he said in flat reply. "You'll have to get each other back to town…Get moving. I don't want to leave her out there by herself. She's only got one arm. She can't fight like that, and I can tell you can't fight at all…so let's get moving."

"I…Y…Yes…" stammered the young woman.

She stepped lightly and awkwardly on bare feet, stepping over the dirty concrete floor of the bunker toward the entrance and exit to the place, stepping around the still twitching, bleeding bodies of the dead and dying cultists that had just tried to sacrifice her through ritual torture.

James shook his head at the sight of her bare white butt. He was getting too old for this life anymore.

He followed her out to the burnt-out cityscape and led her to Sofie. The injured Death Fairy looked up at them both and quickly stood, wiping her eyes free of tears with her remaining hand.

"Rescued this one from cultists," stated James. "She'll help you get to town."

"What!" asked Sofie. "What do I do now? I've lost everything! All of my friends are dead, and…and…"

She stared at the healed stump of her right arm, her lower lip quivering.

James frowned inside his helmet, though these two couldn't see that expression. He had been planning on just sending them on their way, but now…well…there went his pocket money.

"Here," he said quickly. "Take this before I change my mind."

He reacted out of the semblance of a heart, though he did not want to.

He pulled forth the small black box with the pendant, dug around in one of his interior jacket pockets, and then pulled forth the deck of playing cards. He handed them both to Sofie, placing them carefully in her remaining hand, and gave her an encouraging nod.

"You can get a cyber-rune replacement for that arm," he said firmly. "Contact Lazarus Radditz in Coco City. He'll hook you up with some buyers for those if you mention my name. Tell him James sent you. You'll make a hell of a lot more credits from him than you would have from this joint."

"But that's State prop—" started Brenda.

"You…" said James with one gloved pointing finger.

He touched her forehead, and her eyes wandered upwards toward his finger, her face a mask of confusion.

"Get a different job," he said firmly. "One that doesn't involve breaches or dancing."

"B…but…" she stammered.

James directed Brenda's attention toward Sofie by forcefully turning her head.

"Get her to town first," he said roughly.

James looked over toward Sofie and nodded once directly at her.

"You get her some clothes," he said firmly. "And you…"

He once again turned his attention upon Brenda.

"At least tie those rags around yourself," he said. "It's not safe to walk around naked, especially here in Bask. You saw what those mercs were like. You don't need that after what you've just been through."

He stared at Sofie and frowned, though he knew she couldn't see his expression.

"You get a different job as well," he said. "After you sell those artifacts, you can both contact Isha Corkson. She'll get you some safer work…Look, life is terrible enough. I know you two don't know each other, but you will soon, because neither one of you is making it back to Bask without the help of the other, so I suggest you work together. This place is clean for now, but I wouldn't stick around."

The young receptionist tied what was left of her clothes around her waist and chest as she nodded in acceptance, but James had already known she would agree to his commands. Nearly being sacrificed to an elder god through ritual torture had probably changed her mind about any loyalty to the State.

"And both of you get a shower," he said as an afterthought. "Get that blood off…and remember the names I told you…Coco City, Lazarus Radditz, and Isha Corkson."

"What about you?" asked Sofie. "You're just going to leave us?"

"You don't need me," said James with a shake of his head. "Death follows me around like a bad penny. Just get out of here with those artifacts before I change my mind."

Last Breach Rule: Never pick up strays. It hurts too much when you lose them.

They stared at each other as he walked away. They were two strangers who were going to have to rely on each other for survival, but that reliance was something the world needed right now, and that something was trust. Trust was a commodity in short supply anymore.

He left them there after that, content that they would find their way back to Bask. They would have to lean on each other from then on, but he already knew they would.

James walked off in a southerly direction. He'd been south before, and he felt like heading back that way again, maybe contact old friends, have a drink, and shoot the breeze.

Yeah, he'd wasted ammo here, broken a sweat, and gotten his hands dirty with no credits to show for it, but he had something better than credits now.

He pulled forth the item he'd received from the Djinn. It was a genuine, brand-new, rift-charged smartphone, and the best part about it was that the service was both free and infinite. No charges here, money or battery-wise.

He pressed the button on his steel neck collar that retracted his helm so he could enjoy his new prize with his own eyes. His helmet deactivated and retracted, and he blinked and wiped his dark eyes as he stared down at his new phone.

He turned on the phone and waited for it to boot up, and then he went online, that phone reaching across dimensional lines to connect to some other world's internet. It had been many, many years since he'd connected to the internet, but he remembered how to work the device just fine, and he was pleasantly surprised at what he found.

The first thing he did was bring up a funny cat video.

#3…ANIMAL INSTINCT

It's retro-progressive!

Dale hopped up onto one of the empty cafeteria's central tables. He sniffed the air and smelled food, though most of that scent was rotten. It was a good bet there was still edible food, though. There had to be some things still in wrappers somewhere, maybe some canned stuff.

Brittney hopped up next to him, lowered her nose to the table, and sniffed around. More than likely, she was smelling the same garbage he was, but Dale was not concerned with her at the moment. He was busy struggling to remember something.

"K…K…Kitchen…" he grunted.

Brittney grunted in return and hopped down from the table Dale was still crouched upon. She made her way around the weeks-old corpse of a college student, hopping over the body with practiced ease. Dale followed her because he knew she was headed toward the kitchen place he had dimly recalled in his memories.

He skirted around a number of dead bodies, students who had suddenly died from the bad time three weeks ago. He had dim memories before that time, memories of himself and Brittney in something called a "dorm," maybe an "apartment," but that life was a million years gone in his mind, so those memories no longer mattered.

He watched Brittney snatch up a honey bun still freshly contained within its protective plastic shell. She greedily tore open the wrapper, but Dale could not allow her to just wholly devour such a prize.

He jumped upon her a second later, and she spat and clawed at him, but he bared his teeth and growled until she laid back and exposed her bare throat in compliance. He snatched the bun away from her as she whined in protest, but he tore it in half, intent on sharing.

They both wolfed down that prize and continued onward toward the kitchen. Such a morsel as a honey bun was rare anymore, true, but there were greater treasures lying in wait for them within the cafeteria-kitchen place, the place where the old times had prepared food.

Brittney ran ahead of him on light toes and nimble fingers, running on all fours as she hopped over rotting bodies here and there. Dale was used to the smell of corpses, and he knew Brittney was as well; they had been avoiding bodies for weeks now.

Their clothes had seen better days, but at least they still knew how to wear clothes, and this was good, because it was difficult for Dale to think clearly about anything anymore. Neither one of them wore shoes; there was no longer any need for footwear. Besides, he couldn't feel the ground beneath his feet while wearing such strange things.

Brittney hopped over the serving counter, and Dale followed her into the stainless-steel emporium that had once been the cafeteria kitchen. A quick survey of sight and smell revealed a few staff bodies in the place, but there was edible food here; Dale could sense it.

Brittney stopped halfway into the kitchen and perked her head up in surprise. She waited in stock silence, her bright eyes wide, her dyed-blonde hair a wild mess around her beautiful face.

Dale growled as he took in the strange scent, that scent of a rotting corpse but not quite rotted enough, a sweet but dead smell that spiked his adrenaline and swiveled his head toward the threat.

A corpulent lunch lady of middle-aged years stiffly moved from her position against the corner of the kitchen, that corner to Dale's immediate right. This woman's face was a mass of dissolved flesh, her nose missing, chunks of cheek and forehead hanging loose, the eyes white orbs of dead calm, that perfect calm that only came from the rotting ones.

This walking corpse trundled toward the pair in a groping, wobbly stance upon two fat rotting legs. She reached forth with her disgusting melted arms, those arms ever reaching outwards, the white of bone visible upon them.

They were on the fat corpse in a heartbeat. Dale took towards the legs of this woman as Brittney dashed upon the serving counter and then leapt upon the lunch lady's putrefied head and shoulders.

The melting zombie was knocked down in a flash of fury as Dale swept out both fat, gross, decaying legs from under it, pulling back with primal strength as Brittney's momentum and weight took the disgusting thing to the tiles of the kitchen floor. The corpulent woman hit the tiles with a heavy thud, and then the pair tore into her with clawing fingers and instinctive rage.

Dale ripped across the stomach of the lunch lady, pulling apart her dirty smock and the stained white shirt beneath it, and then he tore into the soft, melting flesh beneath that.

Brittney tore at the neck as she used the weight of her bottom to keep the right arm off of her, her clawed fingers tearing and pulling into dead flesh softened by time and ravaging disease.

Entrails spilled out and were pulled forth as Dale savaged the midsection of this walking flesh pot, and Brittney grabbed the thing's left arm, swiveling it down toward its own gnashing, biting teeth.

This once living person chewed upon the dead flesh of its own left arm as the wild pair tore it apart in like fashion. These things were difficult to kill, but once they had suffered enough punishment, they stopped moving for good. Dale knew this, and he knew Brittney knew this, so they worked in unison for this ultimate outcome.

They growled, grunted, and barked as they turned the lunch lady into a pile of irony's own cafeteria mystery meat.

Dale reached into the bloodless cavity he had ripped open and cracked the spine just above the pelvis, pulling some of it forth as he did so. Brittney hopped forward, spun so that her back was against the wall, placed both bare feet upon the fat shoulders of this thing, and pulled on the head until it came free, the fat, grotesque left arm still inserted in the now bodiless head's gnawing mouth.

The corpse stopped moving after that, and both of them left it there, uninterested now that this threat had been disposed of.

Dale sniffed the air, but he was covered with the sweet and sickly scent of the grotesque former lunch lady, so picking up the scent of food would not be possible until he bathed in the outdoor fountain again. They both bathed in the fountain quite often; their natural stink was offensive to both of their sensitive noses.

Nevertheless, they searched the kitchen anyway. There were large cans of food here, huge things that were meant for big crowds, so they grabbed a couple of cans and ran, intent on taking their prizes home. Food was difficult to find anymore, so this was a boon for them both.

They made their way back to their safe haven, the promise of food already at hand.

✶✶✶✶✶

Dale still knew how to do some things, though he did not know why. One of these things involved opening cans with his can opener, something he had learned to do a long time ago. Even so, opening the huge can of refried beans with his can opener had taken some work, but he had managed it.

He and Brittney were now back in their room, and they ate out of the can with their spoons, something they also still knew how to do, use spoons, mainly because it was not as messy as eating with their fingers.

They would eat as much as they could before the contents of the can spoiled. There was no refrigeration anymore, but that was fine. They would find more food somehow. Life was all about finding food and having a safe place to eat that food, and they had both, so this was fine…for now.

Dale walked over to the device he had kept and not smashed. Some things he had smashed, but the device he had not. The device made sounds, comforting sounds, and he liked to listen to those sounds after he ate. It helped him sleep.

The device worked because of these small cylinders he could put in it, things he knew were called "batteries," but his device was old, so he was careful when changing them out. He had plenty of these batteries…They were easy to find in many abandoned places. Nothing but the dead existed in those places now.

He knew that he had gotten this device from his father a long time ago, and his father had acquired it when the man had been young like Dale, so this device was very old, but it still worked, and that was all that mattered.

He turned on his device and played with the knobs on it until he heard the comforting sounds he liked so much, those sounds called "music." The sounds were sweet, soft, and soothing, and such sounds worked wonders on Brittney. The young woman did not remember as much as Dale did when it came to the old life and the old ways, so keeping her calm was a priority.

Brittney fell asleep on the floor a couple of minutes later, the young woman clutching a soft blanket close to her chest.

Dale sat back on his sleeping space and rested his head on his hands, content to just listen. The sounds brought back strange memories, times from another life, but they also brought back good feelings, and that was why he listened.

He closed his eyes for a second, but they snapped back open as the comforting sounds turned to talking sounds. They sometimes did this, but he ignored them…The soothing sounds would come back on their own after a short while.

"And now for your midday survival information," came an older male voice over the device. "Remember to travel along backroads when heading toward your nearest shelter. Avoid major cities, and do not attempt to visit a hospital, clinic, or pharmacy. The infected dead congregate in these areas.

"The shelter closest to you provides food, medicine, and supplies. For directions to your closest shelter, contact…No, wait. We are receiving reports of a new mutation within the virus…

"Some people that are infected are carriers that have not become the roaming dead. These people have regressed. They've gone feral. They should be considered extremely dangerous. I repeat, some people are infected carriers, and we do not yet know if contact with them will spread this new mutation…"

Dale ignored the voice until the comforting sounds played once more. He knew these sounds were called "music," so he closed his eyes to them in order to drift off into some semblance of restless sleep.

*****

Dale's eyes snapped open at the sound of a shout, and Brittney hopped up from her sleeping position on the floor and growled. Something was going on outside.

Dale leapt up from his sleeping space and peered out the window of their little room, their little room on the third floor of an apartment building on what was once a college campus, designations that were meaningless now. Their little room was their safe haven, and that was all that mattered anymore.

Dale carefully studied the debacle going on outside.

A young couple in their mid-twenties was in the street below, but they were on the north side of the building, and that side was swarming with the dead, the dead ones that smelled wrong. Dale and Brittney never went to the north side for that very reason, but now they definitely had a reason to.

Dale barked out a command as he zipped to the door of their little place, and Brittney followed him without argument. They had not seen any others since their internment with the dead here, that time three weeks ago, but now...now was different.

They rushed down the stairs, Dale in the lead. It was going to be tricky getting to the couple outside, because the dead, though slow, were persistent and always hungry.

They hit the ground floor running, pattering along the carpeted hallway on bare feet. There was no way Dale was going to let this opportunity pass them by; there was no way he was going to let the dead waste this gift set before them.

Dale barked out another command as he opened the heavy metal door that led out into the street. He already knew Brittney knew what to do, because they had used this strategy before. It was a skirmisher tactic, one meant to confuse, slow, and/or halt the enemy.

All they had to do was herd the couple back to the doors of their building. The roaming dead, the ones who smelled wrong, only attacked what they could sense, so once this couple was inside the building, then the dead would go away.

Dale dashed into the street, targeting a line of individual dead that would open up a path for the couple to retreat through. He chose his first target, a male, a shambler dressed in a grey suit, a grey suit tattered by neglect and the environment.

Dale rushed behind the walking corpse and used both arms to sweep the thing's legs. It fell to its back as it was struck at high speed, the back of its head splattering open all over the asphalt of the street as it impacted the ground with severe force.

He could see through his peripheral right the swift shape of Brittney leap upon the back of another of the dead ones, the young blonde using the full weight of her body to bring it to the ground. That corpse slid upon the pavement, leaving a gross trail of melted flesh as Brittney momentarily surfed upon its back.

It was easy to ambush these things when their backs were turned to you.

Dale swept the legs out from another one, and then another, and then another, and those walking corpses fell one after the next as he cut a swath through the crowd, making a beeline for the terrified couple in the street.

The male of the couple in the street swung a large green backpack at a swiftly encroaching zombie, but then he took to running, pulling his female mate with him by her hand.

The strangers ran through the gap that Dale and Brittney had cleared, so Dale pitched into a run back towards the building, that building that declared safety, Dale leading the couple towards his and Brittney's own brick and glass haven.

Brittney zoomed ahead of Dale, flung open the heavy metal doors to the building where their haven lay, and then all four of them disappeared within, disappearing into the carpeted hallways that made up this forgotten campus architecture.

The male of the new couple turned and peered through the heavy glass square that constituted a small window set in one of the metal doors.

"They're backing off," he panted out. "They're confused. They're…They're going away."

Dale already inherently knew this. He had known the dead outside would lose interest once everyone living had disappeared from sight.

The male stranger turned and eyed Dale for a brief second as he spoke, but what he saw did not register in his brain before it was too late.

"Thank you," he said as he caught his breath. "I'm Eric. This is Tawnya…Oh…Oh, my God…"

These two did not look like Dale and Brittney. These two did not have dark, animal noses, they did not have sharp teeth, and they did not have a sheen of fine fur covering their pale, peach skin.

Dale had been like Eric once. He had sported the pale, peach skin and the eyes that did not see well in the dark…but that was before the time three weeks ago. Now Dale had a sensitive nose that was dark and bumpy around the nostrils, he had yellow eyes that could catch the slightest glimmer of light in the dark, and he had a coating of light-brown fur all over his once furless, peach body.

The female of the couple did not look like Brittney, either. This female, "Tawnya," had the light, furless skin like Eric. She was not like Brittney, who had a coating of black fur over her own once-peach skin.

But that could be remedied.

Dale was on Eric in the fraction of a second. Now was the time to catch them off guard, especially the male, as the new couple was not expecting an attack.

He leapt upon this "Eric," slamming him against the doors, only to fling him to the blood-orange carpet below. He bit down into the male's left wrist, biting around the cuff of a dark-blue jacket in order to taste flesh, just enough to draw blood, just enough to mix that blood with his own saliva, but not enough to crush bone.

This "Eric's" blood tasted clean, untouched by disease, something Dale had been looking for ever since he had awakened to new instincts three weeks ago.

The female, Tawnya, screeched as Brittney bit into the left side of the young woman's exposed neck. Brittney bit deeply enough to draw blood, just deeply enough to taste it, just enough to spread her saliva through blood as well.

The new female ran down the hall after that, Brittney chasing after her.

The male of the rescued pair struggled to his feet and ran after his own mate, Tawnya.

Dale eagerly chased after him, feeling the thrill of the hunt race through his veins. These two strangers needed to be herded/rounded up into a safe space in order to give the bites time to do their work.

These two, this new male and female couple, would become like them, like Dale and Brittney, wild and free. The male would learn to hunt for food like Dale, the female would learn to sense danger like Brittney, and they would all form a small pack that could search beyond the confines of this limited campus ground.

Of course, the pair of strangers could simply die before they changed. If that were the case, Dale knew they would not become the rotting dead like the ones outside. No, they would simply die, and that was a source of fresh meat neither Dale nor Brittney could pass up.

Yes, Dale would lead the other three toward more of these "clean ones," and then their pack would grow. Their pack would grow, and then that pack would carve out a territory of their own, one free of the still-moving dead.

This was an easier form of procreation, one that involved a faster means of getting what Dale needed. To hunt and to reproduce was what drove him now anyway.

It was, after all, animal instinct.

#4...OBEY

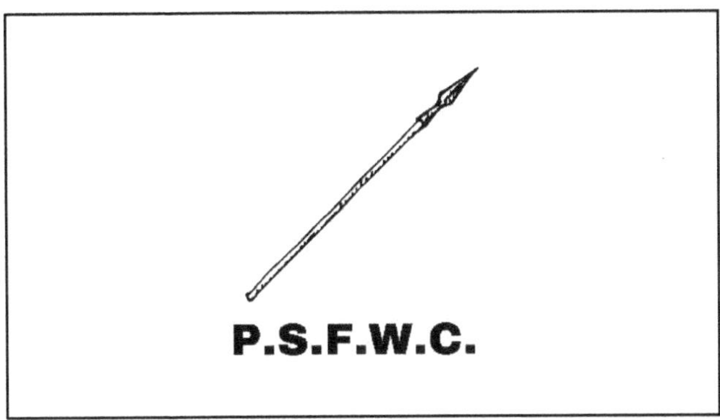

Obey is a four-letter word.

Christoff stood at attention with the other eighth-graders in his class. They were currently lined up in a rectangle of six rows, five students in each row, all lined up on the practice field outside the main body of the school campus.

Mr. Jonas, their activities teacher, marched back and forth before the first line, Christoff's line, the man's shiny whistle jangling on a chain across his pristine white T-shirt marked with the blue-spear logo of the Patriot School for Wayward Children.

The man adjusted his blue ballcap and then blew his whistle, the sound shrill and telling in the morning silence around them.

"What is the meaning of your life!" sang Mr. Jonas in a drill-sergeant's metered tone.

"To serve and to obey!" sang back the class, including Christoff.

"What are the three rules of your life!" sang Mr. Jonas.

"Obey, obey, obey!" sang the class.

Mr. Jonas blew his whistle one more time and then swiveled sharply to his left, and the class followed suit, every student swiveling to match his motion, swiveling to their rights from their viewpoints.

They all turned to view the small group of people watching them, that group consisting of several large men in black suits and black shades, but the man leading that group was an older gentleman in an expensive grey suit, a man with greying hair around his temples, rectangular spectacles upon his hawkish nose.

Two of the men in black suits held large cardboard boxes within their arms, but Christoff did not know what was in these boxes, though he was curious to some degree.

"Attention!" yelled Mr. Jonas.

Christoff stiffened, hands at his sides, waiting in automatic heed of that order. He was now at the back of the rectangle in the last line, as his position was always number one when facing west, but now he was facing north, so his viewpoint had changed.

The important-looking man in the grey suit nodded once as if giving his approval of the professionalism of Class Three.

"Proceed," said the man in a blank, disaffected tone.

"This is Mr. Alexander Patriot!" yelled Mr. Jonas in his drill-sergeant tone. "He is the owner and C.E.O. of the world's largest pharmaceutical company in the world! He is a multi-billionaire with connections all over our *looovely* little planet, and he is the one that provides the food for you little blank slates every single day of the week at our happy little school!

"He provides your clothing here! He provides your instruction here! He provides this wonderful school for you! You will treat him with respect! You will worship the ground he walks on! You will obey his every word if he gives you a command!...Am I clear, children!"

"Sir, yes, Sir!" yelled the class, including Christoff.

This important man, this "Mr. Alexander Patriot," stepped forward and nodded once.

"You are an important contribution to this world," he said firmly. "You have drive, you have initiative, you have commitment, you have purpose, and most importantly, you obey. Those without these five principles cannot succeed in today's modern society. We call these people 'losers.' You do not want to be losers, kids."

He nodded once towards Mr. Jonas.

"Let's show them what happens to losers, Mr. Jonas," said Mr. Patriot.

Mr. Jonas stiffened and nodded in reply.

"Sir, yes, Sir!" he said quickly.

Their activities teacher swiveled on his sneakers to point the class towards the west end of the practice field, and the class followed suit.

Christoff waited at attention, his hands at the sides of his blue gym shorts, his figure standing proudly in his own pristine white T-shirt with the blue-spear logo of the Patriot School for Wayward Children displayed upon it.

He was fourteen now, but he was also the oldest in his class, just in front of Dasheena, who was a mere month younger than him. They were grouped by age, so Christoff was the leader of Class Three, and he was proud of that fact. He would not fail Mr. Jonas. He would not fail the Patriot School for Wayward Children. He would obey.

The class waited in obedient attention as a light-grey bus with black markings drove onto the practice field, that bus driving in from the west.

"Here come the losers, children!" yelled Mr. Jonas. "Carefully observe their mannerisms, markings, and disobedient behavior so that you do not end up like one of them! Am I clear, children!"

"Sir, yes, Sir!" shouted the class.

"Their speech is foul, their behavior is foul, and their very presence is foul!" yelled Mr. Jonas. "They do not what, class!"

"Obey!" yelled the class.

Christoff enjoyed yelling "Obey." He enjoyed obeying. It was his favorite part of existing.

"They do not what, class!" yelled Mr. Jonas again.

"Obey!" yelled the class.

"They do not what, class!" yelled Mr. Jonas one more time.

"Obey!" yelled the class.

"These scum of the earth engage in pointless violence!" yelled Mr. Jonas. "They defile their bodies with permanent ink markings! They partake in unsafe drugs and consume vast amounts of alcohol! They engage in sexual relations before entering the holy sanctity that is matrimony! They rob, rape, and steal! They murder and molest children! They are society's losers, and you are not losers, class! You are not losers because you do what, class!"

"Obey!" yelled the class.

"You do what, class!" yelled Mr. Jonas.

"Obey!" yelled the class.

"One more time and louder!" yelled Mr. Jonas. "You do what, class!"

"OBEY!" shouted the class.

Christoff could feel his adrenaline spike in excitement. He could see Dasheena out of his right peripheral, could see her dark hands trembling at her sides as she vibrated with that same excitement, a tempo of primal essence steeped in blood rush.

The light-grey bus pulled up and parked before them all. The doors of the bus swiveled open, and four large men in black protective riot gear stepped out, each armed with shotguns, each with black helmets and clear visors to protect their heads and faces.

Christoff did not know what was going to happen, but he could feel something important building up inside him, building up inside everyone in Class Three.

A line of ten men in orange jumpsuits walked off the bus in single file, those men chained together in handcuffs. All of them were different, of course, some tall, some short, different ethnicities amongst them, some bald, most of them with tattoos, but they all exuded that greasy aura of "loser" about them, and just being within eyesight of them made Christoff shake. It made his vision turn red.

Mr. Jonas swiveled to his left to point the class's attention back towards Mr. Patriot.

The wealthy and powerful man nodded once to the class before addressing them again.

"This is an important day for you all, children," said Mr. Patriot. "This is the day where we compare your mettle with that of the common loser…You are above the rabble that infests our society!…

"Now, Mr. Garret and Mr. Parnsborough will provide you with your declaration of obedience. This declaration is a contract with society. It is a contract that promises you will be a law-abiding and productive citizen that will contribute to the health and well-being of our nation and, therefore, our entire world."

"Did you hear him, class!" yelled Mr. Jonas.

"Sir, yes, Sir!" replied the class.

Two of the large men in black suits that had accompanied Mr. Patriot, the two men holding the large cardboard boxes, walked through the class, both men handing out something that had been previously stored within their boxes, handing out one identical mystery item to each student.

One of the large men handed Christoff a long, black, metal cylinder, and Christoff eagerly took it, resting it in both hands, the ebony cylinder laid horizontally across his palms, just like everyone else. He held the cylinder this way because he felt that he was supposed to hold it this way, though he did not know why.

He stared at the back of Dasheena's spotless white school shirt, and she stood at attention, true, but he could tell she was trembling with barely contained rage, just like he was. These "losers," these men in orange jumpsuits, enraged Christoff to no end because they did not obey, and he inherently knew this, as did Dasheena, as did the rest of the class.

"What you hold in your hands is the key to our project," continued Mr. Patriot. "This is your declaration of obedience."

"I gotta declaration for ya!" yelled one of the men in orange jumpsuits.

The other men in orange jumpsuits laughed, and Christoff struggled to ignore them. Mr. Patriot ignored them altogether, visibly unconcerned with their presence, a testament to Christoff that the man was truly powerful.

"All of you come from poverty-stricken, abusive, neglectful, and broken homes," continued Mr. Patriot. "You were all flagged by your previous schools as being 'high risk.' That 'high-risk' flag was an indication that you would all become losers one day, but by declaring your obedience to society, all of you will now be successful in life. You will all be winners…In fact, you could even become a giant among men like me."

"That's not what your wife said last night, Patriot!" yelled the same heckler as before.

The men in orange jumpsuits roared with laughter.

Christoff could not contain the swiveling of his own head to view the perpetrator in question. He swiftly turned his head to the left, but he was not the only one. The entire class broke protocol and swiveled their heads in unison, every student searching with burning eyes of hatred for the heckler that kept interrupting their school patron.

The perpetrator was a large bald white man with a short black mohawk on his head. This man was big, over six-feet tall, and he was a mass of muscle with a concrete block for a face. Christoff had absolutely no fear of him, though. This man was a loser, and losers were only good at one thing: losing.

The laughter from the line of men in orange jumpsuits died down as they looked upon the burning hatred radiating from the rectangle of students before them. Christoff could sense a spike of fear from some of them, a black aura of doubt seeping forth, but this did not surprise him. They had every right to be afraid.

"Attention!" yelled Mr. Jonas. "Eyes on Mr. Patriot, children! He is not finished!"

The class, including Christoff, swiveled their gazes back upon their benefactor.

"This is your shining moment, students!" said Mr. Patriot in a louder voice, a voice filled with strange, tremulous excitement. "Thanks to years of research in developing the special vitamins you are given every day, and thanks to your special training here at the Patriot School for Wayward Children, you are a cut above the common rabble, a stab above the normal John and Sally citizen, and you are certainly, most extensively, a slice above the losers of society!...You are all winners...You will be the backbone of our great nation, for you...are...society."

Mr. Patriot spread out those last three words for emphasis, and Christoff let those final three words sink into him, embracing them, letting them merge with his soul. He felt compelled to stand at the ready for action, and he could tell that the rest of the class was ready as well.

Mr. Patriot nodded once toward Mr. Jonas.

"Proceed," he said with a cold smile.

Mr. Jonas immediately swiveled to his left again to face west toward the line of chained men in orange jumpsuits.

"Attention!" he yelled.

The entire class swiveled to mimic his motion.

Mr. Jonas stepped backwards toward Mr. Patriot, towards the group of men all dressed in black.

The guards from the bus moved away from the line of men in orange jumpsuits, clearing distance from these "losers" of society.

"You…are…society!" yelled Mr. Jonas.

Christoff straightened once more and felt a rush of adrenaline flow through his veins. The entire class vibrated like a taught piano wire, something Christoff could sense so much as see. The special training he had received here at the Patriot School for Wayward Children was burning in his blood, and he was ready to show off that training. He could tell that the rest of the class was ready to display their skills as well.

"Embrace your declaration of obedience!" yelled Mr. Jonas.

Christoff acted without thinking. He gripped the black cylinder within his hands and pulled it apart at the center, withdrawing the carbon-steel blade within it. The unsheathing of the blade was multiplied by the sound of all thirty weapons being drawn at once, a loud and audible "SHING!" that echoed throughout the practice area.

"Eliminate failure!" yelled Mr. Jonas. "Go!"

He blew his whistle and made a chopping motion toward the line of orange men in jumpsuits.

Christoff shouted along with the rest of the class as the rectangle of students charged in unison at the line of chained men, these "losers" that had infected the world with their toxic presence.

Christoff paired with Dasheena as they covered more ground than the others, both running ahead of the class, their legs hammering a tandem beat, their footsteps mashing grass as they dashed forward. They both leapt upon the nearest chained man relative to their starting position, and then chaos erupted, chaos and blood.

Christoff sank his blade deep into the man's chest as Dasheena stabbed into the left side of the prisoner's neck. Blood sprayed in all directions as the two students swiftly and brutally made short work of this "loser," stabbing, cutting, and slicing as their blades sank deeply into mortal flesh over and over again.

A third student, Gerty, a short, skinny girl with blonde hair, stabbed into the man's legs and groin as this loser in orange screamed out a bloody death rattle. Christoff had not even noticed her with them, but this did not surprise him. It was Gerty's duty to obey.

The ten chained men in orange fell in rapid succession, three students on each, knives flashing with blood spraying, but the largest of them, the musclebound man with the short mohawk, fought to keep the class off of him, but his desperate struggle was to no avail.

The class moved as one like a school of ravenous piranha, closing in on the heckler from all sides, their blades sinking into his muscle and flesh as easily as scissors cutting through paper. The last prisoner cried out a loud, high-pitched wail as he disappeared beneath that eddy of students and knives, and then there was silence on the practice field, silence save for the class's own heavy breathing.

Christoff reacted to the sound of the whistle, his body moving automatically. He ran back to his previous position to stand at attention before Mr. Jonas, briefly realizing that his spotless, white, school T-shirt was no longer spotless, or for that matter, white.

His clothes and skin were splattered with the dark red of human blood, and one brief and subtle inspection of his two nearest classmates showed them to be models of the same horror show. Dasheena's clothes were in no better condition than his were, and even Gerty's blonde hair was crusted over with sanguine splotches here and there.

This bothered Christoff, but only for a second, and he did not know why it bothered him. It was a pulling of something from deep inside, a remembrance of a prior time when this would have bothered him, should have bothered him, but ultimately, he cast these doubts aside. It was his duty to obey.

Mr. Jonas swiveled to face the stern, yet somehow mocking, form of Mr. Patriot, and the class swiveled in imitation of his action, moving as one like that proverbial school of fish.

"With this declaration of obedience, you are now productive members of society," said Mr. Patriot with a cold smile. "We will continue to monitor your progress…Mr. Jonas…onto advanced training."

Mr. Jonas swiveled to face the class and blew his whistle, and the class swiveled to face him in response to that shrill call.

"We will head to the showers, you will be issued new uniforms, and then we will start advanced training!" yelled Mr. Jonas. "It is time to start learning firearms and electronic espionage!...Attention!"

"Sir, yes, Sir!" yelled the class.

"What is the meaning of your life!" sang Mr. Jonas in his metered, drill-sergeant tone.

"To serve and to obey!" sang the class.

"What are the three rules of your life!" sang Mr. Jonas.

"Obey, obey, obey!" sang the class, including Christoff.

Christoff enjoyed yelling "Obey." He enjoyed obeying. It was his favorite part of existing.

#5…HELL HATH NO FURY

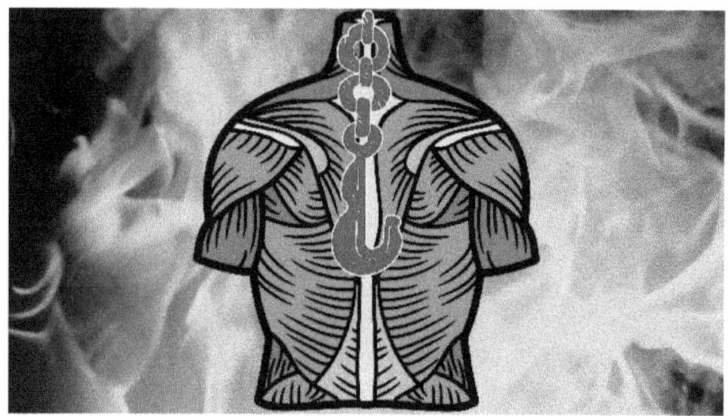

There is both madness and method to her scorn.

Michi stood as the world around her blurred into view. There was pain, there was suffering, and then there was this.

The stones beneath her skinned feet were burning to the touch, but she ignored this due to sheer agony and confusion. She stood upon a narrow path of charred rock and ashen stone, a lake of fire all around her, the flames searing in spurts from the boiling water that bubbled and spat for as far as the eye could see.

The path she was on led out of this boiling hell toward a bare plane of red rock and broken stone spires, a crimson wasteland that wandered away towards who-knew-where.

She was naked, of course, if you could call it that. She had no skin, just muscle and tendons, as if someone had yanked off her protective outer layer or, perhaps, been very careful with an extremely sharp knife.

She staggered forward down the path, ignoring the pain as best she could. This place was hot, so hot that even if she'd had skin, she would have boiled in her own sweat.

The screams around her were deafening, a screaming that bubbled up from the lake of fire that was split by this stone path, and she could see shapes in that lake, vaguely-human forms that reached and struggled for the surface.

She noticed the shape of something massive overhead, a shadow that clipped the orange-black sky, and she looked up for a brief second to see that shape, an enormous ebon thing that lurked far in the distance, but if it had seen her, it did not show it.

There were no words to say in her head. Michi knew where she was, and she knew why she was here, but she was not about to stay here. There had to be a way out, and she was going to find that way out, one way or another, that play on words now forming in her mind, the first cohesive thought she'd had since waking up.

"*Oooout…*" she spat.

Her voice was graveled over, her mouth dry as if stuffed with sand, but she could still form words, and that was good. It was an assessment of sorts, an understanding of what she had left to work with. She had no skin, no hair, no clothing of any sort, but she still had two arms and two legs, two hands and two feet, and that was good enough…for now.

She traveled down the path set within the endless, burning lake, and she traveled that path until she reached the red rock and crimson stone of the wasteland that had previously been on the horizon.

Traveling that path had taken an eternity, so long that she could not remember its start, but she had kept her eyes ahead, always ahead, never taking her eyes off of that horizon, her rage and her fury the engine that kept her skinned legs moving, kept her skinned feet stepping forward. She knew what she had done in order to be thrown down here, but she would do whatever it took to get out.

How she had reached the red wasteland beyond the lake, however, she did not know, as that horizon had never seemed to pull any closer, but now that she had reached it, she would journey forth, looking for a way out. It felt like hundreds of years had passed, or maybe it had only been a few minutes, but it mattered little in the end, because she was here now, and from here she would travel onward, looking for a way out, always looking for a way out.

She decided to start with one of the twisted stone spires of crimson rock near her. She would search every single one until she found what she was looking for, something, anything to guide her out of this place. She was, if anything, methodical.

She did not make it far before a group of others came into view.

These things were not like her…They were hunched over, grey and gnarled, a group of vaguely-humanoid creatures with black eyes and wide mouths full of sharp fangs. They bounded on all fours, bounding toward her with no good intent, and their leader, one slightly larger than the rest, swung a long rusty chain with a sharp hook attached to the end of it.

The big one, the leader of these ghouls, threw the chain as soon as he was within a few meters of her.

"He" was a misnomer, as "it" was a more appropriate term for these things, because upon viewing them up close, Michi could tell they had no discerning characteristics of male or female; they were withered husks of mottled grey, snarling beasts launching forward on spindly limbs and clawed, oversized feet and hands.

Michi caught the hook of the leader's chain with her right hand, or rather, the hook pierced through the muscle of her right hand, but still…she had caught it.

She raced toward the beast to gain ground, putting slack in the chain as the creature bounded forward, but it had not expected her to attack, probably because she was a woman, something still obvious and visible despite her lack of skin.

Michi grabbed a short length of chain with her left hand and garroted the leader of the pack as it tried to leap upon her. That rusty chain wrapped around its gnarled and spindly neck as it hit the red earth beneath them both, and then she pulled up as she booted it to the ground, shoving her skinned right foot into the small of its twisted back.

She pulled up hard as she choked out a malicious laugh, because there was nothing in her but pain and rage, but that combination was more than enough to hear the satisfying "CRACK!" of the creature's neck as its spine snapped.

She did not stop there. Michi reached around with her pierced right hand and hooked the ghoul by its upper jaw, pulling up once more, her fury only increasing, fueled by the madness around her. The top half of its mottled-grey head peeled off a second later, a tearing of sandpaper to the audible ear, and then she suddenly had the chain all to herself, a weapon all her own.

The other ghouls, no less than ten of them, looked upon her with visible fear, because there was something different about their would-be-victim, something not like the others they had feasted upon…or tortured…or whatever it was they had planned to do.

Michi ripped the half-a-ghoul's head from the hook in her right hand, and then she yanked out that hook, that sudden pain a reminder that she was still in control of her own fate, that she was still in need of a way out, and that she was going to find that way out no matter what.

The hole in her hand sealed as a layer of new, pale, peach-brushed skin formed around her right hand.

"Yeeesss…" she hissed out in a dry, sibilant whisper.

She wrapped the long end of the chain around her skinned waist and swung her new weapon in a circular arc, a spin in preparation for throwing, her skinned feet marching steadily forward toward the nearest ghoul.

These creatures backed away at her toothy grin, unsure and unsteady in their countenance, but this proved to be a mistake, as Michi now understood a new rule for this place, but she needed to test this rule just to be sure. She was, if anything, methodical.

She rushed the closest ghoul and swung down hard with her chain as soon as she was within striking range. The rusty hook of her weapon slammed down into the back of this thing, knocking it to the red earth below. She reached down and buried the hook within its mottled back, and then she pulled upwards and backwards as she laughed, embracing the power of her fury and insanity, insanity the last remaining weapon in her arsenal, true, but a powerful weapon at that.

The spine of this creature tore upwards and outwards, ripping through its paper-thin skin, and the skull of this mishappen beast came with it, no blood to speak of, just a puff of dust as the rest of the thing fell to the ground like a partially deflated balloon.

Michi laughed again as her left hand spread over with new skin, new nails upon her narrow fingers.

This methodical research in killing was proving to be more beneficial than just self-defense.

She swung her chain's hook in an arc, and the spine and skull attached to it shattered as they impacted upon the temple of yet another one of these ghouls. The mottled thing went down to the scorched earth beneath her skinned feet, but new skin coated over her right foot as she beat this thing with the chain until its own skull caved inward and its spindly bones broke in visible sections.

The others ran. These creatures, these grey ghouls of twisted limbs and malformed faces, ran in a scattered, panicked burst in all directions, pawing the ground as they beat a hasty retreat.

"*Ruuuun…*" hissed Michi.

She would find them later if necessary, but they were too fast for her to catch on foot. Even so, they had done her a favor in more ways than one, and that was good. She had a plan now, at least one that formed around deliberate action and her new weapon, and that was good.

She continued her journey towards the closest spire of red rock. She was nearly upon it when twin bursts of flame erupted from the sky, two pillars of bright-orange fire that scorched the earth from some sort of blast from above.

Two shapes appeared from out of the flames as the fires died away, those flames gone as quickly as they had come.

Michi stared at the naked couple, one male, one female, as they both pushed off from the red earth beneath their skinned hands. They were like her, but they were also unlike her.

Both of these people screamed in agony, and even with a lack of skin upon their rent faces, Michi could tell they did not have the semblance of mind or the singular purpose she possessed. No, there was nothing but terror and horror and pain on those faces of muscle and tendon, two screaming masses of agony and despair etched upon living human portraits.

She knew what to do, though, so she started with the male. The male was the more immediate threat, after all.

Michi stepped forward and wrapped the chain around his neck, pulling hard with the fury that drove her so, stepping upon his skinned back until he was forced down upon his bare, skinned chest. She snapped his neck as easily as a twig, and then she beat upon his head with the hook until his skull caved in, a splattering of brains and blood that flew everywhere, a fitting action satisfying to her own newfound lust for carnage.

She pulled away the chain, stepping away as his body burst into flames, his body burning away to nothing but ash.

Michi cried out in strange ecstasy as a pleasurable pain ran over her arms and legs, new skin growing over the exposed muscle that tortured her so. It was like the ripping off of a scab but in reverse, a sensation so strange that she had no words to describe it. Both arms and both legs were now coated over with the pale peach-white that she had been so used to in life, and this was good, but there was still more to repair.

The female of the former couple screamed and screamed as Michi walked towards her. This woman was more than likely in shock, understandable for the situation, but this only helped Michi. It made things easier for her, because the female would not fight back while in this state.

Michi whirled her chain and swung the rusty weapon in a low, pitched arc, and the hook of the chain buried itself in the unknown woman's jaw, right above her neck. This snapped the female's mouth shut with a chattering of ivory teeth, a spurt of blood erupting from between those trapped ivory pegs.

"*Ssshhhh…*" said Michi.

She pulled on the chain, pulling her victim forward on skinned breasts and belly, and then Michi stepped around to the back of this poor woman, pulling up on the chain as she planted her left foot into the small of the woman's skinned back.

"I need you…" grunted Michi as she strained hard, pulling upwards with all the might of an untold amount of rage burning from within.

Her victim folded in half as the woman's spine snapped, this female's neck tearing open in the front to gush out blood in an arc, the attack tearing off most of the head from the neck due to sheer viciousness.

"Yes…" whispered Michi.

The woman beneath her bare foot burst into flames, and Michi backed away as the body turned to ash and then blew away in a nonexistent wind.

Michi moaned as her eyes fluttered from the strange, enjoyable pain that washed over her. Her lower half up to just beneath her sternum coated over with fresh skin, and this felt good, addictive, like a powerful drug, but that sensation was just a pleasant byproduct of what she really needed, to be whole again. She sensed she needed to be whole again in order to find a way out, and she was already halfway there.

"More…" she said to herself.

She understood now. The two she had preyed upon were not dead, no. They had gone elsewhere, to the lake of fire, and they would suffer in there before they were taken out and tortured elsewhere. That was how things worked down here.

She needed more, though. There was a way out, and she knew this for a fact now, but she needed more, because there was indeed a way out. She had a metaphorical path to follow in order to get there, and she would follow it, because she was, if anything, methodical.

Michi looked back towards the lake. Lightning crashed across the orange-black sky above, a crackling of raw, purple electricity that briefly lit up the immeasurable surroundings of this terrible plane.

There, in that raw light, was the king of this place, a shape so large and so dark that it was indescribable in measured thought, and in its huge, ebon and clawed right hand was a black, wrought-iron cup, an enormous drinking mug that it dipped into the burning lake, that endless lake of fire it effortlessly waded through.

This creature of vast and evil power flipped the contents of its cup upwards, and streams of fire burst out from the huge container to rain down far in the distance, raining down somewhere on the other side of the lake.

Those were lake dwellers raining down, and she needed them to get more, but Michi could not go that way. She could not afford to have eyes that large upon her. Still, she needed more, and she would get more…somehow.

She headed back toward the spire of stone she had originally targeted. This was really the only path she had so far, so she would take it. She had some skin now, about half, but she knew the key to escaping this place was finding the other half, or earning it, rather, and she would do that…one victim at a time.

It took her some time to reach the spire of twisted red stone, but she had no other encounters along that uneventful journey. This was disappointing in a way, but her investigation had only just begun, so her disappointment was merely a tantrum, something she could easily ignore.

The spire of red stone held no features at first, but then she spied an opening in the rock at the base, a cliffside part in the crimson stone that rent the broadside several meters upwards, a tear in the edifice that could only be seen once up close.

Michi walked up to the opening and peered into the darkness.

A globe of red light split this opening, and behind it was a little face, that of a child, a small boy of four or five, that boy with actual skin and ragged clothes and a smudged face. The small globe of red light hovered within the palms of his dirty hands, lighting the darkness just enough to see the bare earth of a swept red path that led inwards and downwards.

Their eyes met, and the boy ran, running down that dark path into further darkness, the orb lighting his way in a crimson sheathe around his small, pale figure.

Michi followed the boy. There was nothing else to do anyway, and she needed to know why he was here, why he still had his skin and clothes, or perhaps, how he had attained them.

She journeyed down into the darkness, down along cut stone steps into ever-reaching black, following the bobbing orb of red light in the distance.

She stepped into an open space, inherently sensing the change in area around her.

The orb stopped in place, the little boy standing in one spot, and Michi could tell that this open area beneath the spire led upwards through its interior, like the hollowed-out insides of a twisted eggshell.

"Little boy..." grunted Michi.

She walked towards him until she was within a few meters of his small, shadowy shape.

The grand hall before her lit up with crimson light as the red orb flew upwards into the darkness above. The boy ran off to his own left, her right, but that was not what held Michi's attention. It was the huge and fat form of grotesque flesh that grabbed her vision, that blob of disgusting evil menacing an aura of pure malice within the interior of the spire.

The demon before her was indeed huge, not so large as the titanic form of the king over the lake of fire, but this thing was a giant, nonetheless. It was all stomach, two large, fat arms at the shoulders above that huge, burnt-orange belly, and its face was a round ball with slits for eyes, that round ball sporting a maw several meters across, giant fangs in that maw, its fearsome countenance topped by huge black horns spanning from its grotesque, bald head.

This, of course, had been a trap, and she had walked right into it.

Hands and chests and open, screaming mouths attached to terrified faces pushed and strained against the flesh of the spire-demon's belly, those lost souls struggling in vain to escape the engorged stomach of this thing.

The spire demon reached forth with one massive, clawed hand, that clawed hand reaching down towards Michi, an attempt to pick her up and swallow her, no doubt, but it overreached, clearly expecting her to run, a bad habit it had picked up by swallowing its many victims in the past, a bad and fatal habit that Michi capitalized upon.

She rushed it, clutching the rusty but sharp hook of her chain in her right hand. If she could see the faces and hands of its victims in its flesh, then that wall was thinner than it ever needed to be, and considering her rage, her fury, it was far too thin for its own good.

The giant hand came down to grasp nothing but darkness, because Michi was already at the base of its gluttonous belly. She buried the hook into the flesh directly above her head, felt that sharp tip poke through to the other side, and then used her weight and fury to rip downwards, pulling with both hands on the chain to tear open a huge hole that spilled skinned, slowly digesting souls out in a wave of trampling feet, this stampede followed by a sea of green digestive fluid that gushed out onto the red stone of the spire's grand hall.

The massive creature roared out as it shuddered in its death throes, collapsing in on itself, its own weight its greatest enemy, and many, many skinned people, some of them melted down to near skeletons, ran past Michi, running toward the exit that led back out into the wasteland above.

Michi was not concerned with them. She had quickly skipped to her own right, the direction the little boy had fled, dancing to the right to avoid the inevitable explosion of souls and fluid that had gushed forth mere seconds before.

A new regeneration struck her all at once, and she shuddered as more skin coated over her back, her chest, her breasts, and her neck, that strange concoction of pleasure and pain holding her in place for just a few seconds, but she recovered from this masochistic sensation, and now?...Now there was only her head and her face left to fix, and she knew just how to do that, knowing exactly who and what she had to destroy in order to do so.

She caught him cowering off to her right, cowering against the wall as she walked up to him, and she swung her chain in lazy, menacing circles as she did.

"Stop!" yelled the little boy in his tiny voice. "Don't hurt me! I'm just a child!"

"Liar…" hissed Michi. "There are no children in Hell, demon."

The little boy stared up into her still-skinned face, his brown eyes two pools of pleading innocence.

"Please!" he begged. "I am a child! You can't kill a child!"

Michi smiled, a toothy grin unhindered by lips or mercy.

"Don't you know why I'm here?" she asked. "I killed my children, little one."

"What!" asked the boy, his brown eyes widening.

Those brown eyes changed to twin pools of infinite black, his teeth sharp fangs for just a split second, and he spit forth one last hiss, that hiss a resounding cry of defiance, but that hiss ended with the swift and sudden impact of a sharp and rusty hook.

She made short work of him.

The ones who resided here, the ones that tormented those who were forced down here...Their bodies did not burn to ash. No, they just rotted, a fitting end to what they were and had been.

Michi gave a wide grin as her face restored itself, her beautiful face growing new skin over exposed muscle and tendons, black hair growing in all the places it needed to be, and she was whole again, whole once more, ready to continue on.

She knew what to do now, the last bit of understanding open to her. Killing the gluttonous demon and its servant had opened something up, opening up pages in a dark book that she now read in her mind.

She clutched the darkness over the body of the boy and pulled outwards with both hands. A rift of light appeared as the darkness tore open, and Michi struggled to keep the rift open, to make it wider, to make it wide enough to squeeze through.

She cried out as she used the remainder of her unholy strength to push through the rift, pushing through it into the light, pushing through the opening as if being born again, a painful process that was neither pleasurable nor wanted, but it could not be helped. It was rage, fury, and will that had taken her this far, and they would take her further yet.

She forced herself into the light. She had found the way out at last.

＊＊＊＊＊

Michi's eyes fluttered open to fluorescent lights and the beeping of a hospital monitor.

She was stiff from inactivity, but how long she had been here, she did not know.

She winced as she sat up and breathed in and out for a few seconds, her memories coming back to her as her mind crashed in on itself with a strange, otherworldly understanding.

She could remember standing over the little bodies of her two children, blood everywhere upon the hardwood floor, her fingers wrapped around the knife. She remembered charging Giichi as he flung open the bedroom door. She remembered her husband wrestling the knife away from her, and she remembered the pain of that knife sinking into her own stomach and chest as he stabbed her, no breath, her lungs punctured, sinking into black as darkness closed in on her vision.

She lifted the hem of her hospital gown and gazed upon the scars across her belly, but this only angered her further; it only heightened her inner fury.

She was going to deal with Giichi, and this time she would deal with him, because things were different now. She had learned something dark while down below.

She dropped the hem of her hospital gown, shone a cold smile, raised her right hand, and snapped her fingers.

The lights above her popped all at once as the bulbs shattered in unison, cracking the plastic covers that contained them. The monitor beside her bed sparked and crackled with a brief arc of violet electric light before dying as well.

She reached into her hospital bed after that, plunging her right hand through the sheets and mattress as if they were made of water, the material rippling as she punched through the reality of the bed itself, and then she pulled forth a long and rusty chain from that hole, that chain topped by a sharp and rusty hook.

Yes, she would deal with Giichi, but first she would hunt down and kill his entire family…parents, brothers, sisters, nieces, nephews…There could be no stone left unturned, no one left to enact revenge.

She was, if anything, methodical.

#6…Y IS FOR YANOSH

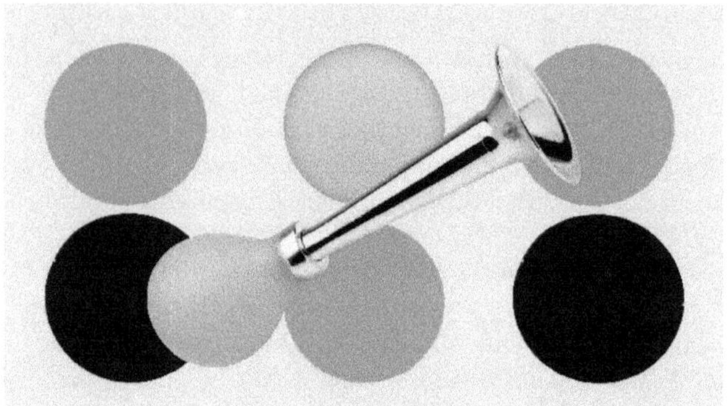

T is for Terror.

Sebestyen sat down next to his little sister, Evike, in front of the television. Sebestyen was smart, so he had gotten the television working again, but it had taken him a long, long time to do so.

He was only nine, but he had grown up quite a bit since the explosion that had destroyed everything a year ago. His father had gone off to work at the factory that fateful day, and the man had never returned, so it was Sebestyen's duty to be the man of the house, though he did not wish to be.

It was a good thing their father had stocked food in the shelter below, their family basement repurposed for just such an emergency. The man had done this for many years, and that paranoia had paid off, because without that food, they would have starved to death within a few days of the explosion.

Their mother had taken care of them over this year, even though everything around them was in ruins. The woman had repeatedly told them it was not safe to go outside, and she had taken care of them as good mothers do, but Father had never returned home, and Sebestyen had come to accept this fact.

The world outside their little house was a smoking ruin, though what had caused that ruin, Sebestyen did not know. They lived in the woods outside the nearest town, so they had been safe from the explosion, but now they were cut off from everything. Isolation had been their father's safeguard, but now it was killing them.

Now Mother was gone, and she had been gone for three days. It had been three days and three nights since she had told them that their food was running low, three days and three nights since she had told them that she would have to go out and look for more.

Now Sebestyen was running the generator. It was something of a no-no, but his mother was not here, and he did not know if she would ever come back, so he would watch the television with Evike until their mother returned or he understood that the woman would not.

Yes, he had fixed the television. He had replaced a bad tube with one of his father's spares, and then it had simply been a matter of fixing the wiring. Sebestyen was smart like that, smart with things electronic and mechanical, and he would have to be smarter still if his mother did not return soon.

"I want Momma," said Evike.

"You say that every day," replied Sebestyen. "I don't know when she's coming back."

Evike's face fell, and he knew she was going to cry.

Evike was only six, so it was Sebestyen's duty to watch over her. It was his duty to make sure she had food and water and safety. He did not like doing this, but it was his duty, and Father had always talked about duty. It was the one thing Sebestyen had taken from the gruff and solemn man.

"We're going to watch the television now," he said quickly. "We'll watch until Momma comes back."

The little girl's smudged face immediately brightened, the response Sebestyen had been hoping for.

He had hooked up the television to the generator. Now it was only a matter of finding something to watch, if there was anything to watch. In truth, Sebestyen did not know if there were any television stations left.

He turned on the huge box and waited for the screen to heat up, hearing the familiar hum of electricity he had so missed over the course of a year.

There was snow on the first channel on the dial, so he turned the big channel knob, clicking from one setting to the next, hoping to have something come through.

"Where is the show?" asked Evike.

"Just give me a second," replied Sebestyen.

He continued to turn the big channel knob until something finally appeared onscreen.

"Here is something," he said firmly.

There was a stage onscreen, a concrete stage with tattered curtains in the back, though what color those curtains were was a mystery because their television was only in black and white.

A jaunty tune picked up along with cartoon noises, and wide letters appeared in sloping curves of white across the screen to match the happy melody accompanying the program.

"What's it say?" asked Evike.

"It says, 'The Yanosh Show,'" replied Sebestyen. "Now quiet. Let's watch."

There was nothing more to be said after that. The show was about to begin.

*****

She was wearing her salmon-pink sweater and her better blue jeans, her traveling clothes, and this simple outfit was accompanied by her thick wool socks and her hiking boots. The weather had been rainy outside, so she had dressed accordingly. She had intended to leave some miles behind her if need be, but that was before she had been caught.

Cili struggled to free herself from the mobile iron wall she was chained to. She wriggled her wrists and ankles back and forth, but the chains were locked in, so there was nothing she could do.

The two guards on each side of her, two big men in black ski masks wearing black T-shirts and blue jeans, kept watch on the stage ahead, ignoring her frantic struggles altogether.

This mobile metal wall was propped up on a small wooden pallet, that pallet propped up upon its own jack, and one bump or hitch in the motion of this pallet could cause the wall to fall forward, squishing Cili like a bug. It was not a happy thought.

This wall had probably been an iron door at one point, but now it was being used as an offering plate, a sacrificial stone that Cili could only guess in its purpose. She had the sense that she was indeed being offered to someone, and what that person would do to her was more than likely not very nice.

A man, if you could call him that, shuffled out onto the bare, concrete stage. He was wearing a tattered and burnt clown suit, a once-yellow outfit with stained green, blue, and red polka dots all over it, and he shuffled across the bare grey floor in oversized, blood-red clown shoes, the kind that were so large, Cili wondered how anyone walked in them at all.

The infernal music that played all around them ceased with a loud clash of symbols, and then the terrible man in the clown suit started into his act.

"Hello, kids!" cried the man. "It's me, Yanosh the Undead Clown!"

The children on the bleachers behind Cili, children she could not actually see due to the restrained position she was in, cheered at the sight of their beloved host.

The horror she felt was unfathomable.

This man, this "Yanosh," was indeed something terrifying. His face was gone; there were only bits of melted flesh hanging off of a white skull, two very human eyes looking out from the orbital sockets, his tongue hanging out of the right side of his mouth through a gap in his broken teeth.

When he spoke, his jawbones barely unhinged, and though his tongue flapped up and down from the motion, his speech was impeccable, something Cili could not understand in possibility, nor did she wish to.

"Today's episode is a special one!" said Yanosh. "We have a real showstopper today, kids! Let's give a warm welcome for our line of exciting new guests!"

The children erupted in cheer once more, but Cili cringed at the sound. There was nothing right about this, nothing sane about this unholy perversion of a children's television show.

Yanosh the Undead Clown pulled forth a small honking horn from a large pocket on the side of his outfit. He squeezed the red rubber bulb over and over again to send forth a "HONK! HONK! HONK!" as a little boy in a striped yellow and purple shirt walked out onto the stage.

This little boy had a round face smudged with dirt, dark circles under his brown eyes, and his torn blue jeans and ragged white tennis shoes had seen better days.

"Tell everybody what your name is!" said Yanosh in an excited tone.

"Mihaly," said the boy.

"Let's show everybody what you can do, Mihaly!" exclaimed Yanosh.

The horrendous clown waved toward someone offstage, and a big man in a black ski mask, this man wearing a black tee with blue jeans, carried out a small wooden coffee table. The man in the ski mask then proceeded to set down that table before the boy and this mockery of a clown.

The big man in the ski mask walked offstage, leaving the pair to do…whatever it was they were going to do.

Yanosh knelt down beside the boy and nodded once.

"Let's show everybody what your gift is, Mihaly," he said quietly. "Don't be nervous now."

The little boy nodded back in return, and then he picked up a butcher's cleaver from the coffee table, the kitchen tool ridiculously large in the boy's small right hand.

"All right, kids!" yelled Yanosh. "It's showtime!"

A drumroll sounded out from somewhere offstage as this little boy, "Mihaly," laid his bare left arm on the table and then raised the cleaver high.

Nothing but a small whine escaped Cili's lips as her eyes widened in frightful anticipation.

The cleaver came down with exceptional force, far more force than any little boy had a right to wield.

Cili gagged as the cleaver sank into the flesh of the boy's left arm, the blade slicing clean through the limb despite muscle, tendon, and bone.

The little boy raised the stump of his left arm, that arm severed past the elbow toward the wrist, but there was no blood. A green liquid spurted from the chopped-off stump, and then the flesh turned a burgundy color as it grew at a fantastic rate. A wriggling octopus tentacle took the place of the missing limb, a long, wine-colored tentacle with visible suction cups along its interior line.

"Oh!" said Yanosh as he backed away, two melted, skeletal hands over his toothy, lipless mouth.

This boy, "Mihaly," raised his tentacle arm and waved it at the crowd.

"That is in…credible!" shouted Yanosh as he honked his little bulb-horn over and over again.

He picked up the boy's severed left arm and waved it at the nonvisible crowd.

"Let's give Mihaly a hand, kids!" he yelled.

The children in the nonvisible crowd cheered long and loud over this foul, profane feat.

The arm within Yanosh's skeletal grasp melted into green goo, dripping through his boney fingers to splatter across the concrete floor.

"Oops!" exclaimed the unholy clown.

The children laughed along with him, but then the boy, Mihaly, laid his new tentacle arm across the coffee table, a mirror to what he had done with his real arm.

"Oh, we're not done, it seems!" yelled Yanosh.

Mihaly raised the cleaver once more, and that kitchen blade came down yet again, chopping off the tentacle this time. The boy raised his severed left arm, and then a new human arm grew back in from the stump, replacing the tentacle as if it had never existed at all.

Yanosh picked up the tentacle and waved it at the crowd, but he did not get to comment about it before the strange limb had melted away into green goo.

"No octopus for dinner tonight!" laughed the clown.

The nonvisible children laughed in unison as Yanosh honked his horn a few times.

"Let's hear it for Mihaly!" yelled the clown. "Mihaly, the incredible tentacle boy!"

He honked his horn again as the children cheered.

Cili felt sick. She wanted to vomit, but she held it in. This was wrong, all of it, so wrong that she wanted to pass out, to fade out for a while, but her adrenaline would not let her do so.

*****

"This is weird," said Evike. "I like it."

Sebestyen tried not to hyperventilate. He did not know what was going on with this show, but it was not normal, which meant the world was not normal anymore. Something very, very bad had happened out there, and he did not really want to know what that bad thing was.

"This is not right," he breathed out.

He reached for the knob to change the channel, but a shriek of protest from his little sister stopped him cold.

"I want to watch it!" cried Evike. "I want to watch Yanosh!"

Sebestyen pulled away from the knob, but his hands were shaky. It was better to appease Evike for the time being than to allow her to stew in boredom and fear, but he prayed that their mother would come home soon, because he was truly scared now.

Sebestyen was nine, but he wasn't stupid. There was no way any channel would have a kids show like this, and this fact scared him, but there was also no way he was leaving the house with Evike to look for their mother. No, the world outside was…was lost.

*****

Cili sucked in her breath as she struggled against her chains.

The madness around her had only intensified as the show dragged on. The guests had included a little girl with spider's legs, a little boy with a giant eye in the center of his forehead, and another little girl with three arms, her third arm sticking up and out from between her shoulder blades.

Cili did not have any words for what was going on here; she only knew that she was in the very depths of

Hell, a pit where no light would shine down upon her forsaken soul, though she did not know what it was she had done to suffer such a punishment.

"Now it's time for the Amazing Jelly Girl!" cried Yanosh.

The undead clown pushed a small cannon out onstage with the help of his masked stagehand. The cannon was comically large and round in the back, like something out of a cartoon, a short and squat thing with a red, wide, round barrel upon wooden yellow wheels.

There was a large paper target set against the concrete of the backstage wall, that target concentric rings of red and white. Yanosh and his stagehand maneuvered the cartoonish cannon until the barrel lined up with the large and bright paper set against the back wall.

The grotesque clown pulled a huge match from his tattered outfit and struck the crimson matchhead against the concrete floor. The pencil-sized match sparked to a flame, and then the demented host used the oversized match to light the big white wick of the comical cannon.

"Let's give a warm welcome to…Jelly Girl!" yelled Yanosh.

The wick burned down until it disappeared into the cannon, and then the cartoonish artillery weapon blasted forth a loud "BANG!" that reverberated around the studio.

A huge blob of purple goo splattered against the paper target, and then that paper sizzled as it melted away, the goo sticking like a great glob of violet snot to the concrete wall behind it.

A face formed in the goo a moment later, a young and attractive female face with distinct blue eyes, and then that face spoke, the lips moving and sounding out words in a young woman's voice, something impossible to Cili but still there all the same.

"Hello, kids!" exclaimed the face within the purple goo.

"There she is!" yelled Yanosh.

The nonvisible children erupted in cheer once more, and the disgusting clown waited until those cheers had died down before speaking again.

Yanosh walked up to the glob of purple goo with a woman's face.

"So, what are we up to today, Jelly Girl?" asked Yanosh.

"Just hanging around, Yanosh!" smiled the Jelly Girl.

The children laughed as the Jelly Girl blinked twice in response.

"You know what time it is, then?" asked Yanosh.

He turned and lifted his skeletal hands, palms up, waving them both upwards in a double motion, a motion of reply from the crowd that Cili could not see.

"It's mail time!" said the Jelly Girl along with the crowd of children.

Yanosh pulled forth a yellowed letter from his rent clown suit.

"This letter is from little Ambrus!" he said in excitement, his tongue bobbing up and down as he spoke. "What does it say, Jelly Girl?"

He held up the letter before the pretty face in the purple goo.

"Dear Yanosh—" started the Jelly Girl.

The children cheered again as Yanosh pulled forth his horn and honked it a few times. He nodded his head in recognition, and the crowd died down once more. He put his horn away and then held up the letter to the pretty face again.

"Dear Yanosh…" continued the Jelly Girl. "When are we going to have another sliming? It has been too long. Your friend, Ambrus."

Yanosh covered his ungodly jaws with both skeletal hands and stamped up and down with both big shoes—left shoe, right shoe, left shoe, right shoe—a stamping of insanity as real as the stamp on the letter he was holding.

"Oh, Ambrus!" he cried. "Do we have a surprise for you! We *are* going to have another sliming! In fact, we will have another sliming…on today's show!"

The children cheered. Yanosh pulled forth his horn and honked it, and this caused the crowd to cheer even louder.

The "HONK! HONK! HONK!" of this demented clown caused Cili to cringe and grit her teeth, and she struggled to free herself from her chains, but her struggles were to no avail.

"Let's hear it for Jelly Girl!" yelled the clown.

The crowd cheered, of course, but Cili had closed her mind to this madness. Whatever was going on with this show was too much for her to process, too much for her rational mind to bear.

Yanosh waved for someone offstage as he backed away from the Jelly Girl.

"Now it's time for our friend, Spackle Head!" cried the clown. "Spackle Head, come on out and do your job!"

"Spa…ckle…Head! Spa…ckle…Head!" chanted the children.

A huge bald man in a black T-shirt and black pants walked out onto the stage, this man carrying a small metal tub. The top of his bald head sported a large fan of flesh and bone in the shape of a putty knife, that fan sticking straight up like a flattened arrow pointing toward the ceiling, something so bizarre that Cili could not take her eyes off it.

This man walked up to the blob of purple goo that was Jelly Girl, bent down, and used his putty-knife head to scrape her off the wall until she fell into the tub he was carrying, a plop of awful significance that Cili heard so much as saw.

"Ooo, ooo, ooo!" winced "Spackle Head" as the flesh of his putty-knife protrusion began to smoke and turn red.

"Sorry!" came the Jelly Girl's voice from the metal tub. "That's the acid! My fault!"

The children laughed as Spackle Head walked offstage with the tub containing Jelly Girl, his bald head still smoking, and Yanosh honked his horn as he stamped his feet up and down again.

"That is never not funny!" yelled Yanosh. "Right kids!"

"Right, Yanosh!" yelled the crowd in return.

The grotesque clown nodded in an overexaggerated way, his tongue flapping up and down as he did.

"Now it's time for the end of our show," he said in a sad voice.

The children resounded out a loud "Awwwww!"

"Don't worry kids!" encouraged the clown. "We'll be back tomorrow!"

"Yaaaaaaay!" yelled the crowd.

"But first, it's time…for…our…sliming!" yelled Yanosh.

"YAAAAAAAAAY!" shouted the children in unison.

The guards on each side of Cili pulled off their ski masks. One had green scales all over his hairless head and face, and the other was nothing but hair, so much so that Cili could not see his eyes or lips.

These two monsters that looked like men took a minute to unlock her chains, and then they forced her toward the stage, a steady marching of doom that Cili could not escape.

"Wait! Wait!" pleaded Cili.

Her two guards led her up a small set of wooden stairs onto the concrete stage to stand before the unholy clown.

"Wait, please!" whined Cili.

"She wants us to wait, kids!" yelled Yanosh.

"BOOOOOO!" shouted the children.

Cili's eyes wandered over the dark shadows that comprised the crowd of this insane children's show. She could see the warped forms of arms, legs, tentacles, and even wings on these children, a mass of growths that should have never existed in nature.

It stunned her into silence, the appearance of this madness, and she found herself speechless, nothing more to say. All she could do was whine in fear at the sight of it all, the image of this looking-glass reflection into Hell.

"It looks like the kids have spoken!" yelled Yanosh. "On with the sliming!"

"Sli…ming! Sli…ming! Sli…ming!" shouted the audience of twisted, mutant children.

The guards backed away along with Yanosh, and Cili was left turning her head in all directions due to a nameless fear, unsure of what was going to happen next.

A drumroll started up offstage as Cili looked toward the twisted host of this show, Yanosh the Undead Clown, but the grotesque man simply pointed skyward with one bony, skeletal finger.

Cili looked up and froze in stark terror.

A massive, dark-green shape surrounded by swirling tentacles, a huge mass covered with yellow, slitted eyes and mouths full of razor-sharp fangs, stared down at her from directly above the concrete stage. A huge orifice opened up in its center mass, this maw a fleshy, gaping hole that dripped a disgusting green goo that splattered down to the floor here and there.

Cili had just enough time to let cry a shrill scream as a putrescent green waterfall spit down upon her, covering her from head to toe in its disgusting ooze.

*****

Evike escaped the blanket surrounding her and placed her hands upon the television.

"Momma!" she cried out. "Momma!"

Sebestyen pulled her back from the large electronic box and quickly turned off the television.

"It's not real!" cried Sebestyen as he held his little sister close. "It's not real, Evike!"

"Momma!" wept Evike in his arms. "Momma!"

"It's not her," said Sebestyen in a shaky voice. "It's not her…It can't be…"

He was shaken to the core, but his fear only heightened as he heard the sound of something huge crawl through the living room doorway. He turned to stare at this intruder, though his subconscious mind knew what he was looking at before his conscious mind did.

"I'm home, children!" came their mother's voice. "Sorry I was gone for so long. It took a little time to get back after what happened to me yesterday, but guess what! I was on a television show!"

This woman's face was their mother's, though it was three times larger than it should have been.

Their mother's face was set within the body of an enormous, fat, flesh-colored worm, and there were large mandibles set around that familiar face, long and brown leg-like things with white spikes at the tips. These mandibles moved in seemingly unrelated motion to each other as the mutant woman slithered her huge, grotesque form into the living room, a sheen of sticky mucus surrounding her.

Oh, no, they did not have to wait any longer. Their mother was home at last.

#7…WYNTER

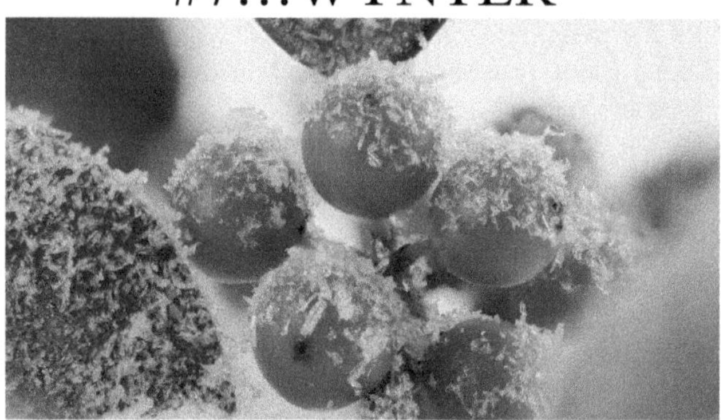

It's horror in Fay English!

Mary stared out the window of Tucker's Dodge Aspen. The trees went by in a lazy fashion as the car sped along, but the brown of the leaves upon the nearly bare wood was depressing in and of itself. The seasons had turned toward winter, and winter was nothing but a downer.

"In Summer whan the forests growe,
And rayn falls round the countryside,
The elder gods of heath and snowe
Doon come upon the countryfolk."

"Yeah, but I liked the last one," said Minnie. "I've seen it twice."

Minnie was Mary's friend from when they had attended high school. The young woman was currently seated on Helen's left, while Mary sat on Helen's right. All three of them were stuffed in the backseat like sardines, but that was okay, because this was their vacation, so a little discomfort was worth it.

"It was stupid," said Tucker. "They had those dancing teddy bears at the end. *The Empire Strikes Back* was better."

This vacation had been Tucker's idea. No one else had thought to use their Thanksgiving break for a road trip, and it beat having to deal with family. All five of them had lied, of course. Their families had heard different excuses from each of them, but their little ploy had worked, and that was all that mattered.

"Well, I'm not watching it," said Helen. "It's been playing since May...since *May*, guys...I didn't want to watch it then, and I don't want to watch it now."

Helen was Mary's friend from college. Tucker and Earnest were friends from college, too, but Tucker was more Earnest's friend, and Earnest was Helen's friend, so this whole trip was more of a collection of acquaintances rather than...well...a group of friends.

"There are some great scenes in it, though," said Earnest. "The battle at the end with the Death Star is so much better than the one in the original. Seeing it on the big screen will just...It will just blow your mind."

"I know," smiled Minnie. "It was awesome. I really liked the first one too."

Mary didn't particularly care for *Return of the Jedi*. She hadn't even seen the original *Star Wars*.

Not that any of this mattered at the moment. She suspected they were lost, though Tucker would never admit it. A strange fog had picked up around the forested scenery passing outside her window, and this was concerning to her, if only because it was out of place.

"Do you know where you're going, Tuck?" she asked out of slight concern.

"What?" asked Tucker. "Oh...uhhh...yeah...I think so..."

"Wait, what?" asked Helen. "You *think* so? What in the hell kind of answer is 'I think so'? Do you know where we're going or not?"

"Yeah, yeah," nodded Tucker. "We're in Missouri, right? That's all we really need to know."

"Uhhh…I think we need to know a little more than that, Tuck," said Earnest.

The young man pushed up his glasses and shot Tucker a concerned look.

"It's cool," said Tucker quickly. "We passed a sign a few miles back. There's a little town up ahead. We'll just stop there and ask for directions. It's no big deal."

"A man ask for directions?" asked Helen. "It's the end of the world."

Minnie burst out laughing at Helen's little dig. Helen joined her in that laughter, and Mary followed suit.

"Yeah, yeah," nodded Tucker with a smirk. "Laugh it up, you harpies."

"Harpies?" asked Helen in facetious anger. "You've got a gearhead and a nerd who've managed to get three babes to come with them on a road trip, and you insult them?"

"Well, you are hot, Helen baby," smiled Tucker. "You know, if there's a hotel in town…"

"Dream on, Tuck," smiled Helen in return.

"Hey, I've got two other babes in the back," shrugged Tucker. "You've got that thick, curly, black Italian hair, and that's hot, but Minnie's a natural blonde, and Mary's got that cute, short red hair…It's not like I only need you."

"*Oooooooo…*" taunted Minnie, but Helen ignored her.

"I don't know about Minnie, but poor Mary, here, is a virgin," warned Helen. "You keep your paws off her."

"Helen…" sighed Mary.

She had not wanted the world to know that, especially if that world included someone like Tucker.

"Fine," shrugged Tucker. "Minnie can accompany me, then. That leaves you with your virgin friend."

"Yeah, well there's always Ernie," said Helen. "He's a good boy…I like good boys. They always wear those tighty-whities that show off their bulge."

Tucker snorted out a laugh, and Helen joined in with him.

"Guys…" warned Earnest in uncomfortable reply.

"Yeah, no kidding," said Minnie unhappily. "Come on…We're not pieces of meat or anything. What's wrong with you two?"

"Yeah, yeah," scoffed Tucker. "We'll behave for n—Hey…Look up ahead."

Mary pressed her face against the cold glass of her window to study the large wooden sign that appeared like a ghost out of the nascent fog around them. The thick wood of the sign was emblazoned with the burnt etchings of the name "Seasons."

"Seasons?" she asked. "That's a town?"

"Eh, whatever," replied Tucker. "We'll just slide in, fill up, and be on our way."

"Nah, nah," said Helen. "We can look for a motel or a hotel here. Maybe this is one of those quaint little villages with an inn. Whatever the case, I'm tired of driving…riding…whatever. I'm tired of being in this car."

"You want a vacation in a little dump water in the middle of Missouri?" asked Tucker. "Seriously?"

"Weren't you the one asking if there was a hotel?" asked Helen. "You're telling me you don't want to stop at a hotel for me?"

"Yeah, but…" drawled off Tucker as visible realization dawned upon his sharp face.

He grinned into the rearview mirror and nodded his head twice.

"Your wish is my command, princess!" he said excitedly.

"Princess?" asked Minnie. "It sounds like you want a cookie."

"A cookie's not what he wants," smirked Helen.

"The seasons fair, the seasons four,
A day of choosyng yn their midst,
Whan Autumn turns to crisped snow,
The peoples give to royals eald,
The kyngs and queens of seasons four."

Tucker's Dodge Aspen rolled into the little town of Seasons.

Mary peered out the window on the passenger side, but something felt off, not right.

There were shops and houses here and there, but they all looked different in style and make from anything else she'd encountered in this state. There were cottages of stone walls and thatched roofs coupled by larger buildings of slate block, something old-fashioned and foreign that did not represent the Midwest houses that normally dotted the landscape out here.

"This looks like a nice little town," said Minnie. "I wouldn't mind vacationing here."

"I don't know," said Earnest in a cautious voice. "The architecture here suggests a throwback to the Middle Ages, but that's impossible…unless this is one of those historical towns…"

"Well, throwback is definitely what this is," said Tucker. "Let's find a gas station or something. This place is giving me the willies already, and we haven't even stopped anywhere yet."

"Yeah…" said Helen quietly. "There's something in the air here…I don't like it."

"Where are all the cars?" asked Mary.

"Outside the world doon they live,
Yn oother realm twixt mortal and fay,
Outside the cares of oother men,
The peoples to the seasons give."

The townsfolk emerged from closed doors a moment later, at least a hundred of them, and Tucker had to slow the car due to the sheer presence of their pressing swarm. These people were dressed in clothing long out of date, long, *long* out of date, and Mary had to blink twice just to take in the sheer ridiculousness of it.

"This is definitely one of those historical towns," said Earnest. "Their clothing dates back to the fifteenth century. I mean, this is something you would see out of the Middle Ages…I knew I was right. Maybe we shouldn't be driving through here, though…"

"Well, you can tell them to get out of the road, then," said Tucker. "I can't drive five miles-per-hour like this…We'll just pass through. Tell 'em we're just passing through, Ernie. If they want us out of here, I can't do it like this."

Earnest rolled down his window, but Mary felt deep down that this was not a good idea. She had a sixth sense about these things, but she did not say anything, not because she didn't want to, but because she was shocked by the sheer antiquity of this town's people.

"A boon ys given on anoynted day,
Whan elder gods lead gift astray,
So peoples braced for chill and snow,
Doon carry out the bidden offer,
Thus fillyng the empty village coffer."

A knife flashed into view as Earnest leaned slightly from the window in order to say something, but Mary could not warn him in time. A large man, a portly man in Medieval garb, trotted forward alongside the vehicle, and in his right hand was a dagger, a steel weapon honed to deadly sharpness upon its double edges.

The crowd swarmed the Dodge Aspen as Tucker was forced to hit the brakes, but all hell broke loose after that. There wasn't even any time to scream.

"The Oak Kyng ys chosen first,
As his reign shal swiftly ende,
And yn that endyng trees lay bare,
As Summer ys banished and Autumn wanes."

The dagger flashed forward and cut loose the seatbelt that held in Earnest. The poor young man could only shout in protest as he was pulled through the open window by several rough hands after that.

Mary wanted to scream, to shout, to say anything at all, but fear had overtaken her, enough fear to freeze her in place, more than enough fear to keep her from doing anything useful. No, it was Helen and Minnie that screeched in her place, both young women shrieking to beat the band, though Mary could not blame them.

"HEY!" shouted Tucker.

He slammed the car in park and reached over to grab Earnest's heel, but he could not hold onto him. Earnest was pulled through the window and into that raving mob, and Mary watched in growing horror as the young man's clothes were roughly stripped from him, all of his clothes, even his glasses, every last article of clothing ripped from him until he was buck naked, shivering in the cold.

Mary did not want that to happen to her.

"Enters nowe the Holly Kyng,
Whose harsh reign ys known full wel,
Wor yn his hand a hammer ryngs,
The soundyng of the wynter byll."

Earnest's door was pulled open, and these hostile strangers entered the car. Three of them tried to pile in at once, large, hairy men with full beards and mustaches, and Tucker tried to fight them off, but they pressed him down to where his struggling was futile. Tucker's door was opened from the inside, and then he was pulled out of the car in shouting, angry protest.

Tucker's clothes were stripped from him until he, too, was naked, and as for Earnest…Mary couldn't even see Earnest anymore. The sea of hostile strangers about the Aspen was too thick, coating everything like a tidal wash of browns and whites.

Mary watched in both shock and horror as her two female compatriots shrieked and screamed in terror. She could see tears forming in Helen's dark eyes, because whatever was happening, it was not something any of them had expected. This was supposed to be their vacation, but…no one actually knew where they were. None of their family members held a speck of a clue that they had even left the campus.

"The Rose Queen ys the byloved oon,
Worshipped for hire fair and grace,
For she coaxes the maiden to call and syng,
Makes wild byasts doon what they must yn spryng."

These mad, crazed people piled into the back, and Mary was finally able to find her voice. She shouted in protest, shrieking like the other two, but Minnie's door was pried open first, and the young woman was pulled out into the tidal throng, disappearing into it as her clothes were stripped from her as well.

Mary could not imagine what that was like for her friend, but she knew she was about to suffer the same fate, so it mattered little. She was terrified, and as much as she wanted to feel sympathy for her companions, as much as she wanted to scream at these people for what they had just done to Minnie, she could only scream for herself.

"And thanne bycomes the Yvy Queen,
Whose reign ends with driftyng snow,
Side by side with hire oaken kyng,
She ys the ember of Autumn's glowe."

Helen's seatbelt was cut, and then she was pulled through Minnie's open doorway, screaming and crying, her hands reaching for Mary in some last-ditch attempt at salvation. It was heart-wrenching, really, but there was nothing Mary could do about it.

Mary ground her teeth as Helen was stripped of her clothing, the young woman disappearing like a pale phantom into the mob, just like Minnie. Mary had seen her friends naked now, something she had never really expected to see in her lifetime, and certainly not under these circumstances. It was really too much to bear.

Of course, she knew she was next. She was the only one left.

"And last the maiden ys brought to byar,
Hair of fire, loyns untouched, unsoiled by manly ways,
The envy of the elder kyngs,
Given fertile ground by the Rose Queen,
Given motherly ken by the Yvy Queen,
She ys the prize twixt Oak and Holly,
She ys the house from whiche seasons spryng."

Mary did not resist as they opened her door and pulled her bodily from the car. She did not even cry out as they tore her clothes from her, though she did not enjoy her body being on full display for all of these strangers to see, nor did she enjoy that biting cold that accompanied a brisk early winter combined with full nudity.

Her arms and hands were forced behind her back as she was bound by thick ropes at the wrists, and she was pulled/jostled forward in a manhandled rush toward some awful destination that she could only imagine in her worst nightmares. There were no words for this horror show in her mind, no expression of thought that was comforting, descriptive, or otherwise.

She was herded toward a small wooden stage in what was probably the center of this little village, a stage where her friends awaited, each of her friends tied to a separate large wooden pole, those poles erected at the back of the stage, that stage pushed against these thick, sacrificial pillars that were once trees.

There were five of these poles in all, but only the center one was bare of any individual. Tucker was tied to the furthest left from the crowd's view, then Helen on his own left, the center empty, then Earnest, and then Minnie last.

"What is this!" cried Mary, but with the shouting and excitement around her, those words were mere motes on the wind.

Her very naked friends each wore a wreath as a crown upon their heads. Tucker's head held the red signature of holly berries entwined in his, Helen's was made of ivy, Earnest's of oak leaves, and poor Minnie's was bedecked with roses, pink roses that were definitely out of season for this chilly time of year.

Mary did not know what any of this was about, but she had seen plenty of movies and TV shows about such things, so this did not bode well, not at all.

It took three large and burly men to force Mary up onto the stage. She spat and kicked and struggled, but they dragged her forward and bound her to the center pole against her will, binding her arms to that pole with practiced ease.

A large bearded man donned a wreath of yellow daisies upon her head, a wreath made from yet another species of flower that was vastly out of season. The wreath was coarse against her soft skin, scratching her slightly, the body of the circlet made from woven sticks of some sort.

"Let us go!" screeched Mary, though she knew such a command would only fall upon deaf ears.

She briefly turned her head from left to right, studying the terrified, horrified expressions upon her friends' faces, the tears that flowed, but there was nothing to be done but wait, wait for whatever terrible thing was to happen next.

"In the bright flames, the spirits dance,
Such merriment they make.
They call forth the harbyngers of seasons' ende,
The kyngs and queens of seasons' ken,
The kyngs and queens of seasons spent."

This mob of raving lunatics stepped forward with lit torches. Mary's eyes widened in complete terror as they lowered those torches toward the bottom of the stage. She had not noticed any kindling under the stage while being led up here, but then again, she had not been in any position to notice such a thing.

The strong, acrid smell of woodsmoke filled her nostrils as the underneath that was the stage lit aflame.

A powerful and terrible sarcastic humor came upon her as she shivered, bare naked, in that cold chill of November wind, an invasive thought that entered the back of her mind and would not let go in its sadistic grip:

At least they would be warm.

The flames licked up around the stage as the insane townsfolk backed away from what was to become Mary and her friends' funeral pyre. These crazed throwbacks watched through the rising smoke, their eyes madness, their hearts as blackened as the burning underneath of that sacrificial stage.

However, the worst was yet to come. The madness was not yet done with Mary, not yet done with any of them, as the roaring fire beneath them was only the beginning.

Four tails of bright-blue light sprang forth from beneath the stage to fly in vivid circles around them, four wisps of brilliant wytchfire that spun and circled before them, four great tongues of blue flame that bedazzled the crisp air and left behind floating spots in Mary's vision.

"In spryng doon the wild creatures call,
Libidynous yn their lust,
To sewe the seeds of Summer,
Yn fertile ground they plant.
The Rose Queen grants hire kisses,
The bucks dance,
The does await their victors' creed,
And the Rose Queen smiles,
Hire power oon of newe life,
Subtle but strong."

Minnie screamed as one of the dancing wisps of bright-blue flame struck her in the chest, right between her small, innocuous breasts. The young blonde went up in a wreath of blue flame, the fires burning up around her like a lit, gas-soaked wick, and then Minnie stepped forward from the pole, the fires dying away, sputtering away as she walked toward Mary.

The young blonde was not burned, no, but one look upon her and Mary could tell that this thing was not Minnie anymore. Mary's friend from high school looked vastly different, the young woman alien in both features and face, though she was still quite beautiful.

The young blonde's face was slenderer, her ears long and pointed, but it was the eyes that both captivated and horrified Mary…They were two orbs of sickly pink, the pupils so small they were mere dots of black, and the combination of such a color with the sharp beauty of Minnie's features caused Mary to shiver and shake from something other than the cold, and that was in spite of the heat emanating from the burning wood and the sting of pungent smoke around them.

This thing that had once been Minnie stepped forward and lightly kissed Mary upon the lips, though Mary was too stunned and horrified to even turn a cheek toward her in defiance. That kiss was electric, a spark of something that plunged deep within Mary, but it was also an atrocity, a gift from an abomination, something Mary did not want, nor need.

Oh, she could feel it in her, a toxic brew of fertility mixed with lust, a gross and out-of-place sensation for such a moment as this. Mary winced at the urgings of it, but her once-friend, Minnie, only smiled a row of perfect, ivory teeth and then turned to walk toward the edge of the stage, flashing her bare backside as if she had no decent care in the world.

The flames licked around the edge of the stage, but they grew no higher, and all the while the mob of insane townsfolk watched through the smoke as three spirits of bright-blue flame danced in the chill air, but those tongues of flame were about to be reduced to a mere couple, because yet another target had been chosen by the azure wisps.

"The Ivy Queen displays hire prowess,
For she ys the mother that teaches hire wisdom,
Passyng forth the Autumn's bounty,
Grantyng yonge brides the gift of birth,
And swete milk to suckle from the teat."

It was Helen's turn to suffer the sapphire flame. She was struck in the chest as well, and then she was a living pyre of cobalt blue, a pillar of azure flame that parted to reveal her nude figure changed, just like Minnie.

The raven-haired young woman walked toward Mary and smiled, though her once flat teeth were now slightly sharper, her face slenderer, her chin pointed, her ears longer and pointed as well, but once again it was the eyes that chilled Mary to the bone.

Helen's new eyes were an ivy green, an ivy green dotted with those tiny pupils, and once again, the person behind those eyes was no person at all; it was something alien that stared into Mary's own naturally green eyes, something not of this world.

Helen reached forward with one long, pointed finger, a sharp white nail on the end of that slender digit, and she touched Mary's forehead, right between Mary's own green eyes.

Mary shook and shivered and cried out as that sharp nail drew blood, but her screeching was not from any pain but from the sudden, horrendous knowledge that was plunged into her. It was more of a feeling than anything else, an essence of the nature of life, all of it, from the hungry growth to the rotting decay, and this shook her, tore her down from the inside out…It was not a pleasant sensation.

"The Oak Kyng strides forward,
Al of Summer at his command,
And byaryng forth a wooden blade,
He summons the weapon to ope hand.
Of power does the Oak Kyng yield,
In Summer's height and heat to wield,
But lavish does the daylight spend,
Markyng Wynter and the Oak Kyng's ende."

There was another flash of azure flame as Earnest went up next as a living pyre. He strode forth toward Mary, his eyes a forest green, unwholesome, his face an elven caricature of what it had once been. His brown hair was a wild and spiky mop, his long ears pointed to match the rest of his slender face, Shakespeare's Puck born into strange reality.

His nude body was muscular now, his now bronze skin smooth and his frame a form of athleticism that belied his former state, and this stirred lust inside Mary, though she did not appreciate the betrayal of her own body. There was a certain alien quality about him that caused her blood to pound in her veins, but this feeling disgusted her to no end. She was a prisoner here, and whatever was going to happen, it was not going to be pleasant; it was not going to end well.

The young man turned and raised his right hand. A long blade of flame-tempered wood stretched forth from his open palm, tendrils of oak twigs wrapping around his slender right arm, oak leaves sprouting from those twigs, and he pointed that deadly weapon toward Mary, forcing her to wince in sudden fear. Mary did indeed feel a shaking fear at that moment, for she was sure he was going to kill her, but he turned the blade toward a naked and terrified Tucker instead.

"The Holly Kyng ynvokes his own name,
His virgyn bride he comes to claim,
For angry ys he at the Oak Kyng's slight,
As Wynter comes with Wynter's myghte.
The Holly Kyng byars a shard of yce,
A sword for the barren neck to slice.
In jealousy he calls the Oak Kyng to stage
So that blades may syng and battles rage."

The last of the blue tongues of fire struck Tucker in his bare chest, and the young man screamed as he went up in cobalt flames. He stepped forward from the flame after that, but his appearance was the most alien of them all and arguably the most terrifying.

He was a nightmare of light-blue skin and sharp, wicked features. His eyes were white like snow, and his pupils were tiny black dots barely visible from a distance. His black hair was spiky like Earnest's, but that was where the similarities ended between the two young men. Tucker's now blue nose was long and pointed, his teeth razor sharp points of ivory death, and he looked wholly evil, wholly disturbing in his open malignance.

He walked up to Mary and grinned at her, though she turned her head to the side out of fear. He reached up in response, turning her cheek to look back at him, and his touch was cold, as chill as any December grave. Nevertheless, there was power in his touch, something awful and terrible that had existed before men had ever walked the earth, and this stirred yet more lust in Mary, something equally as awful and as terrible as the thing that was currently touching her.

She did not like these new feelings that burned within her bare chest, alien feelings that had no place in her world.

Tucker stepped backwards and raised his right hand. A long blade of jagged ice formed from the light-blue palm of his right hand, a sharp and deadly, hideous weapon in sight and make. He pointed the jagged blade at Mary as if in claim, and then he leveled this awful weapon at Earnest.

Mary already knew what this was about…She held complete understanding now. She was the one they were going to fight over. She was the prize that had to be won.

"The two kyngs duel,
Their prize the last of ynnocence,
But al thyngs ende,
And so must Summer
So that Wynter may bygyn."

The two young men, now something else, were upon each other in an instant, their strange and deadly blades flashing, but it was over far too quickly.

Earnest beat down upon Tucker's blade with his own, and Tucker dropped to his knees, but the young man with light-blue skin sliced Earnest across the right leg just below the knee. As the bronze-skinned boy dropped to his right knee, Tucker took advantage of that momentary opening. He stood and sliced across Earnest's exposed neck in a rush of fury, and the college boy's head flew from his bronze shoulders to roll across the wooden planks of the burning stage.

Blood erupted in a fountain from the neck stump as Earnest's finely-honed, bronze, headless body collapsed to the stage.

Mary was horrified, but not as horrified as she was a second later.

Earnest's severed head rolled to the bare feet of Helen, and the nude young woman picked up the head and held it as if waiting for something. Earnest's bloody, headless body then arose from its prone position, walked over to Helen, and took the head from her.

A doorway of light appeared offstage, a portal of brilliance that coalesced into unheralded existence without rhyme or reason, and the mad crowd watching parted to make room for it. Mary could sense that this doorway led elsewhere, somewhere far and away from the cares of the real world, somewhere she had no desire to visit, that no mortal should ever visit, much less stay.

Earnest, still holding his own bloody head in his hands, walked offstage toward the doorway. He took Helen's arm in his, Helen on his left, the young man still cradling his own severed head in his right arm, and the couple entered the portal of light, vanishing forever as far as Mary knew.

Minnie, Mary's longtime friend from high school, turned toward Mary one last time and blew her a strange, sultry kiss. The young blonde then sauntered offstage, swaying her bare bottom back and forth in an almost insulting manner, sauntering off until she entered the portal, disappearing altogether after that.

"The Holly Kyng returns to his land of yce and snowe,
His prize he carries yn his frozen hands,
For yn his castle shal they consummate their bond,
And from this marriage, Wynter ys born."

Tucker's icy sword shattered and blew apart in a flurry of frozen, blood-smeared crystals as he walked up to Mary. He pulled her rope bonds apart as if they were made of dandelion wisps, and then she was swept up in his cold embrace, their nude bodies pressed together as he held her close to his bare, light-blue chest, though she was the only one giving off any heat.

His manhood was already excited, a clear indication of what was coming next, though Mary was not looking forward to it.

She was bodily carried off the stage as the entirety of the village of Seasons cheered and roared over Tucker's bloody victory.

Mary shivered as the inevitable truth reached her terror-stricken brain, filling her with a cosmic knowledge of unwanted understanding. This was what it meant to be Persephone dragged down to the underworld by the sullen god, Hades, to be a bride to a chill corpse of an alien thing.

Tucker carried her through the shining portal of light, and Mary could feel the absolute arctic air pouring through it, flowing over her, chilling her to the bone, though she did not freeze. It was a slow torture of cold that sank into her, but she would not die from it, not ever, and she knew this, even as the light surrounding them blinded her from everywhere at once.

She clutched Tucker tightly to her as his blue feet crunched through crisp snow, their destination a lonely spire of black in the barren distance, that stone spire a singular castle of frigid remorse in a wasteland of frozen hell, a hell consisting of little more than ice and snow gleaming against a clear sky enshrining a bright yellow sun.

Her body turned on her as her newfound desire awakened, her breath a rigid steam that concentrated into crystals before her frost-laden face. She panted in anticipation of what was to come, a terrible mixture of both panic and lust, though this toxic brew was most certainly unwanted.

She was a bride now, married through a ceremony crafted in Hell, though she was not blushing, and only one thought crept across her ice-locked mind at it all, at the sheer insanity of it. That thought was one of helplessness, a helplessness born of things far beyond her control, and even more so, far beyond her mortal understanding:

Oh, yes...Wynter awaited.

#8...THE SALESMAN

Hungry for a sale?

Howard could see the lights in the distance as clear as anything, strange flashings that spread across the pink and orange early-morning clouds. It was that time of the morning between night and dawn, predawn, if you will, or maybe just dawn beginning, but whatever the case, the lights in the sky he was currently observing did not look natural.

"Now, what could that be?" he asked himself.

He was headed in that direction anyway. He had the top up on his Nash Metropolitan to keep out the chill morning dew, he had the newspaper from yesterday right next to him, he had his brochures in the back, and he had his encyclopedias in the trunk. He was ready to start the day, but those lights in the distance stoked his curiosity, so he decided to head in that direction, though, as previously stated, he had been headed in that direction anyway.

There were no people out this way, but he had wanted to see the construction out here, out here near the desert, out here that was to be a suburb of this out-of-the-way little town he'd come to buzz around. Emerald

Cactus was rapidly growing, and that growth was due to a metaphorical goldrush of new factories coming in, the type of growth one could see just about everywhere this day and age.

Emerald Cactus was going to be a whole new area to peruse and/or target. You couldn't be a salesman without a proper sales range to cover, so this growth was good news. Howard had known for some time that this little town was out here, but this had been the first time he'd ever come to call on it.

Even so, where he was headed was the suburb construction zone, but he was only headed there to get a lay of the land…The weird lights were just a bonus.

Dawn emerged from behind him as he drove west. The early-morning light emblazoned everything with its welcomed glow, so it was no surprise when the first of the road signs came into view. It wasn't the signs that distracted him, however. It was the singular house in the distance that caught his eye, a white two-story of brand-new build, a little gem out in the middle of nowhere.

"Must be their show model," said Howard to himself.

He pulled up to the place on this freshly laden road and parked his Metropolitan. The lights he had seen were long gone, but they had originated from this area, originating out where this house had just been plopped down in a lonely spoonful of nothing.

He grabbed his newspaper, exited his car, and took a brief moment to study the trio of billboards across the way.

"Now, that is just tacky," he said with a short grin.

There was a large sign that just said "YES!" along with the profile of a young man, a doughy-faced blond in a grey, three-piece suit. This young man could be seen from the front, from both sides, and from the back, four standing profiles to show himself off, his standing profile splayed across the sign like a jackass, some kind of cockamamie advertising promo that some corporate nitwit had come up with.

There were two other signs besides that one, one on each side of it, one with a picture of the front of a two-story house, the very same house he was in front of, and another one with two shots of the empty interior of that house, an empty living room coupled with an empty kitchen, a barren kitchen countertop in that kitchen, etc. The only thing in common between the signs were the words "Rising Heights" displayed along the bottoms of them, along with a telephone number.

"Huh?" asked Howard to no one in particular. "That is a terrible advertising campaign. Don't these city boys know how to come up with a pitch?...Shameful."

He was busy shaking his head when he both heard and saw motion behind him. The front door of this newly-constructed house opened, and the doughy young man from the billboard appeared at the entranceway.

"Now, hold right there, son!" said Howard in excitement.

He rushed to the back of his Metropolitan, popped the trunk, and pulled forth a fresh set of encyclopedias. He could smell a sale, even to a younker like this one.

He trotted up to the young man in the doorway and smiled, and this young man smiled back at him.

Howard held his precious encyclopedias in the crook of his left arm, his newspaper tucked in there as well, because he knew his trade; he knew it inside and out.

"You're that boy from the sign," said Howard in a matter-of-fact tone. "I take it you are in charge out here?...Well, I can see the new foundations laid out here, but the advertising you people have is a little...well...I'd have done things differently. Let's just leave it at that."

Howard peered past the young man and into the home. It was bare inside, of course, but he wanted a peek-in anyway, if only for research. He was going to be selling in this neighborhood; that was a guarantee.

"May I step in for a moment?" he asked.

The dough-faced young man stepped backwards and aside to allow Howard to step in.

"Much appreciated," said Howard as he tipped his fedora. "I noticed this little showpiece on the way up here, but I was originally drawn to some strange lights in the sky…You wouldn't know anything about that, would you, son? I didn't see your vehicle out there, so I can only assume it's parked in the back, but surely you noticed the flashing lights…Now that's curious."

He had only taken a few steps into the bare living room, but the wood floor beneath him held his attention for a second. His step was a little bouncy, as if the floor were somewhat spongey.

"This floor feels strange," he said more to himself than to the young man. "It feels a little…spongey…This is new wood, right? Shouldn't it be firm? Who is in charge of your construction out here?"

He stamped down upon the supposed hardwood of the floor with his right dress shoe, but a quick tap-tap revealed the floor to be as hard and as firm as it was supposed to be.

"Now that is odd," he said unhappily. "I could swear this didn't feel right a second ago…Floor's made a liar out of me. Oh, well."

He took a brief look around the empty living room, nodded toward the smiling young man, and took a moment to look outside one of the front windows.

"Well, your interior looks exactly like the sign outside," said Howard in thoughtful notice. "Can't says much for the rest of the place yet, but I can say you don't even have a For-Sale sign outside. I know this house is probably a show model, but you should always have some kind of pitch going on. That's good advice for any kind of sales. Don't matter what you're selling."

He turned to stare at the doughy young man, but the young blond simply smiled, a creepy affect that mimicked the sign outside. Nevertheless, Howard was undeterred. Even so, this boy seemed a little…slow. Maybe he was someone's idiot nephew, but whatever the case, Howard knew he could get his point across.

"A For-Sale sign?" he asked. "Like, uhhh…Now wait here. Here's one on this here newspaper I brought with me…Like this…"

He opened his paper and held up a picture of a Sale sign that was part of a hardware-store ad.

"It's like this," he said. "Now you tell whomever you work for that they need a sign like this to attract…"

His words drawled off as he stared out the living room window. Out on the dirt patch of dry land that was going to be a lawn was a new sign, a sign that Howard could swear had not been there a mere second ago.

"Now that is curious," breathed Howard. "Why, I could have sworn…Now wait just a minute…"

He looked at the ad in the paper and then studied the sign outside. The two looked identical, a grey background with white lettering, similar to the ad in every way, right down to the curvy lettering, right down to the loop in the "L."

"Now that is odd," said Howard. "I guess…I guess such a small burg as Emerald Cactus just has a surplus of these signs and whatnot, eh? Makes sense…Surprised I didn't see that sign earlier, though. How odd…"

No matter. He still had encyclopedias to sell, and if there was one thing he understood, he understood that slow people like this boy were easy marks. A little run around of words would get him a quick purchase, maybe even a promise of next year's set as well.

"What I have here in my hands, other than this newspaper…" started Howard. "What I have here in my hands is the greatest supplement to your educational future that you shall ever possess, my boy."

He handed the first book in the set to the smiling young man, but their hands touched, and this was cause for alarm, if only because of the young man's temperature and the moisture clinging to the boy's hand.

"Whoa, there, son," said Howard nervously. "You're burning up. You sure you're okay? Feels like you've got a fever or something. You're all sweaty…You doing all right?"

The young man simply nodded in reply. His expression was unchanging, almost like a doll with a human face, and it was unnerving, but Howard knew better. This young man was simple, so it was no surprise the boy was off in a number of ways. That was how these people were.

"Okay, then," nodded Howard. "All right, then. In your hands is an encyclopedia of extraordinary knowledge, one that no upstanding young man such as yourself should be without…You understand what I'm saying, son?"

The simple young man flipped through the encyclopedia and stared down at its contents with wide eyes. He looked back up at Howard and nodded once.

"Yes," said the young man.

"Ah, well…good," said Howard. "Glad you can put two words together."

"Yes," replied the young man.

"Is 'yes' all you can say, son?" asked Howard.

He was joking of course, but it was the first thing that had come to his mind, so he had said it without thinking.

"Yes," replied the young man.

That reply, of course, was a red flag…This was going nowhere. It was clear to Howard that this boy was a little too simple to be worthy of any sales pitch, no matter how expertly thrown.

"That was a joke, son," frowned Howard. "I can see, perhaps, that my encyclopedias might be wasted upon you. Nevertheless, you must have a caretaker or a guardian that watches over you, might you now? They would definitely be interested in these here fine instructional manuals…You do have a guardian, don't you, son?"

"Yes," replied the young man.

"Good, good," said Howard in return. "Now, look see, son. I'll give you my card, and you can give that card to whoever takes care of…Now…Now that is curious…"

He noticed it for the first time since he had stepped into this show home, and he was surprised he hadn't noticed it before…There was a kitchen counter in the living room.

He walked past the simple young man and into the west side of the living room to inspect the kitchen area, that little kitchen area complete with a white countertop, a sink, and a stove…or at least, half a stove. One half of the stove was complete with burners and a glass window for baking, but the other half was just white metal, just a square block of white, a featureless sham, no cooking implements to show.

"Now, what kind of cockamamie setup is this?" asked Howard. "Why, you've got the kitchen in the living room, and what's the matter with this stove? It looks like you just built the place based off the sign outside, like you just ripped off the image and pasted it…onto…"

He walked back into the main area of the living room and peered out the window. The sign outside was made of two separate pictures, one of the living room and one of the kitchen, both merged together with an indistinct line. The stove was on the right half, the kitchen half, but only half of said oven was shown on the sign, cut off from the rest of the picture.

"What in the blazes kind of setup is this?" asked Howard. "I'll have to call that number outside and chew on someone for this kind of sloppy craftsmanship. That there puts an insult on anyone in sales. You got a simple boy as your showman and a halfcocked house that looks like it was designed by a circus clown. I don't know what kind of jackass setup you've got going on out here, boy, but I think I'll be on my way."

He reached for his encyclopedia, gripping the edge of it, but the young man would not let go.

"Now, son, I need my book back," warned Howard. "Let go, now. I told you…I have to be on my way now."

He yanked hard on the book, but he could not pry it loose from the simple boy's grip.

"Let go now!" cried Howard. "Let go, I say!"

The young man's doughy, smiling face bulged with visible veins, large, thick, dark-blue, pulsing veins, and his dark left eye spun in its socket, spinning from right to left, spinning to show nothing but white behind it. A sheen of moisture congealed upon the young man's rapidly reddening skin, almost a mucus in texture and quality, something more than disturbing enough to rattle Howard's own previously unshakable nerve.

Howard immediately let go of his encyclopedia and backed away. Something was terribly off with this place, something awful terrible, so it was time to duck out and accept his losses, even if that retreat meant losing one of his precious encyclopedias.

"I see I've m…made a slight error," stammered Howard. "You can keep that book, son. I'll just be on my way."

He tipped his fedora out of habit and quickly walked toward the front door, but the door slammed shut in his face, slamming shut on its own as if pushed closed by a giant, invisible hand.

"What in the blazes!" yelled Howard as he gripped the doorknob.

He twisted and pulled hard on the knob, but then he let go of it as realization set in. The knob did not feel like metal, no. The supposed metal felt warm to the touch, hot almost, but sweaty and squishy, fleshy, to be exact.

"What in the name of—!" asked Howard in growing shock.

He turned to address the young man, but he stood stock still in frozen terror as the boy's form morphed into something truly terrible. The young blond was all pulsing flesh now, like an overgrown tongue lined with blue veins and red arteries, the grey of his suit and the blond of his hair merging in color with the darkening reddish hue of his mucus-coated skin.

"My God!" yelled Howard.

He turned to find some way out of the barred door before him, but the white of the door had glossed over with a clear mucus, the door itself changing, transforming into a reddish color, it too lined with blue veins and the red of arteries.

The floor tilted as it sloped inward, the center of the living room opening up to form a pit that convulsed and slimed over with that same clear mucus, the floor itself turning into a spongey, fleshy surface that quickly became a slippery hazard for footing of any kind.

Howard dropped the encyclopedia set he held within the crook of his left arm, letting slip free his newspaper as well. The books slid down into the opening maw before him, the newspaper turning wet and ruined as it touched slime, and then he was sliding, sliding down this tilted floor into this pit that had appeared out of nowhere.

He understood too late that the mucus covering everything was not mucus at all…It was saliva, and this house was no house at all. No, this showpiece of supposed wood and mortar was something entirely else, something clearly not of this world.

He screamed as he dropped into the pit of a giant esophagus, but he could feel the burn of an acidic cloud melting through his clothes and burning his skin even before he dropped bodily into a great pool of caustic stomach acid.

✳✳✳✳✳

Diedre exited through the passenger's side of her son's Chevrolet Bel Air.

They had spied this lonesome white house out here in the construction area of Emerald Cactus, and there was already a car parked outside, a red and white Nash Metropolitan, so it was clear someone was here.

"I just want to take a looksee, Jimmy," she said firmly. "This must be a showhouse for the project. I want to know who Mr. Cawson hired to sell our houses. Get an eyeball on our mouthpiece, you know. We won't be here long."

"Yes, Mother," replied her dutiful son.

Her son was a doughy, blond boy of fairly handsome make, not exactly Charlton Heston or James Dean, but he was as good as any to be a spokesmodel for the project.

"Your face is up on that sign, Jimmy," said Dierdre. "You need to smile. We're taking a risk here, so I want you to be on your best."

"Yes, Mother," replied her son.

"And 'yes' is right," said Dierdre. "That's our catchphrase. We want that 'yes' out of new home buyers, you hear? You just follow my lead from here on out. Understand?"

"Yes, Mother," sighed her son.

"Don't you sass me, now," warned Dierdre. "We're just here to see if—"

She was cut short as the door to the lonesome house opened wide. A clean-cut man in his mid-thirties, a clean-cut man in a brown suit with a matching brown fedora on his head, stood within the open doorway and waved them forward.

"Well, hello, hello!" he called out. "Visitors are always welcome!"

"I'm Mrs. Danforth!" called back Dierdre. "I own this here property! Did Mr. Cawson just put you on?"

"Yes, yes," nodded the man as he tipped his hat. "Why don't you come right on in!"

"I hope you have credentials," said Dierdre as she walked forward, her son following her right behind. "We want Rising Heights to be the premier suburb of Emerald Cactus, and I need to know if you've got the gumption and grit to sell my properties."

"That I do, that I do," nodded the man. "I was a little uneducated in the past, a little wet behind the ears, but that has changed recently. I came into some literary works that have vastly improved my knowledge, and I picked up a lot of sales techniques from a…mentor…you could say. Digested all of his knowledge in one go."

"You don't say?" asked Dierdre. "Well, why don't you give me the rundown, Mr…"

"Angler," nodded the man. "You can call me Mr. Angler."

"Fitting," smirked Dierdre.

"Just step on in, and I'll make a little lunch," smiled Mr. Angler. "I haven't entertained a female as of yet. I'm wondering about your tastes."

"I have standards, Mr. Angler," warned Dierdre. "Those are my tastes. You had better not disappoint."

"Oh, one of us won't be disappointed," smiled the salesman. "I'm sure your tastes are exquisite. In fact, I'm looking forward to them."

He stepped aside, waving both hands in an arc as a signal for them to enter.

#9…COLD

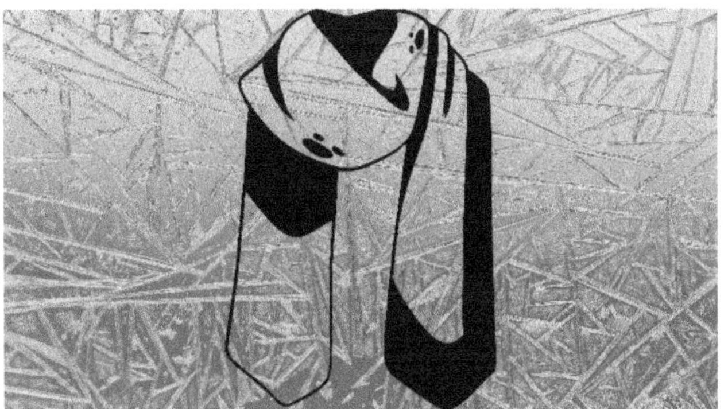

When Hell freezes over.

"Thanks, guys!" called out Andy.

He waved goodbye to his two best friends as they crossed the street. They were on their way back to their own lives, but still, their help was much appreciated.

He still had his moving van to return to the rental place, but that could be done later. For now, he was just going to relax in his comfy chair and watch some TV. The last of the big furniture had been delivered and placed, so now it was time to sit back, watch the game, and down a cold one.

He walked to his new fridge, pulled out a beer, and twisted off the cap. His new IT job was still plaguing his mind, but that little problem would be remedied shortly with a few swigs and the start of the baseball game on his new flatscreen.

Andy was twenty-five and just starting out, but he knew he had a bright future. In fact, things were already going his way. By some miracle of amazing fortune, no one had rented the incredibly-cheap bottom apartment in this little two-story, and the only other occupant in the building was an ancient crone of a woman that supposedly lived in the upstairs apartment, but he didn't know anything about her, nor did he need to.

"Don't rent, don't rent, they all said," he scoffed as he parked his butt in his brown comfy chair. "What a load of crap. Why should I buy a house yet? The landlady can be in charge of all the repairs and stuff. I don't need to add any more responsibilities to my list of duties."

He flipped on the TV and went straight to streaming on a sports channel. He was an avid baseball fan in the summer and a rabid football fan in the fall. Of course, there was always basketball or hockey, boxing when he could catch it, MMA whenever, and even volleyball if he felt like it. He had his priorities, but he could watch them all.

He would have continued with his mental love for sports, but he was interrupted. In fact, he had only taken one sip from his beer when the doorbell rang.

"Oh, come on…" he groaned as he set his beer down on his coffee table.

The doorbell rang again as if in urgent request, so he decided to hoof it. The faster he addressed whomever, the faster he could get back to the game.

"Coming!" he called out as he trotted to the door. "Hold your horses!"

He opened the door to reveal the intrusive presence of Mrs. Gorman, the landlady.

"Oh," he said quickly. "Hello, Mrs. Gorman."

The woman was in her early sixties, but she was pleasant enough, if not a terrible gossip at times. She liked to talk, but Andy wasn't one to be rude, so he inevitably listened, even if he didn't want to.

Mrs. Gorman stepped inside without being asked and closed the door behind her.

"Hello, Andy," she said quickly. "I just stopped by to see how you were settling in."

He had been settling in just fine, at least until she had interrupted that settling process. Nevertheless, she had accepted him as an occupant, and he knew which side his bread was buttered, so he was not about to rile her in any way.

"I'm doing okay," said Andy with a sheepish grin. "How are you?"

"Fine, fine," said Mrs. Gorman. "Listen, I just came by to go over a few things."

He had expected this, of course. It made sense that she would want to warn him about parties and drugs and late-night noise and all of that crap. It was the standard runaround for any renter. Even so, he'd already gone over all of this with her.

"Okay," said Andy warily.

"You should already know the rules here, so I won't go over them again," nodded Mrs. Gorman. "I don't need any property damage, but I expect a nice young man such as yourself won't have any problems with that."

"No, no," said Andy quickly. "Nothing will get damaged."

"Also, I know you may want to have a woman over here," said Mrs. Gorman, "but you should inform me first if anyone else moves in with you."

"Of course," nodded Andy.

His girlfriend lived in her own apartment. She was working on her doctorate at the local college, and her apartment was within walking distance of the school, so there was no point in her moving in with him, at least not yet…Yet another reason not to buy a house yet. They both needed to save their money.

"Also, there's one more thing," said Mrs. Gorman in a nervous tone.

"Yes?" asked Andy.

"You should…try not to disturb Mrs. Arkle," said Mrs. Gorman.

"Is she the lady that lives upstairs?" asked Andy.

It was a valid question. He had no idea who Mrs. Arkle was.

"Y…Yes," said Mrs. Gorman nervously.

"Oh, I won't bother her," said Andy. "If she asks for any help or anything, I'll be sure to help her out."

"That's…not a good idea," said Mrs. Gorman.

"What do you mean?" asked Andy.

He was curious now. His usually talkative landlady was being unusually guarded, and this was cause for both alarm and interest.

"Does she have some kind of infectious disease or something?" he asked. "Should I be worried?"

"Not exactly…" frowned Mrs. Gorman. "Let me ask you a question, young man."

"Okay," nodded Andy. "Shoot."

"Are you religious, Andy?" asked the older woman.

He was not sure how to answer this. The truth was and always had been that he did not have a religious bone in his body. His parents were Methodist, but he'd ditched ever going to church a long time ago.

"Uhhh…not exactly," he said cautiously.

"Well, I'm sure you'll find religion when you're older," said Mrs. Gorman. "In any case…I just wanted to say…I'm not sure how to put this…Do you know how old Mrs. Arkle is?"

"No idea," shrugged Andy. "All I've heard from a few people around the neighborhood is that she's really old. I didn't even know her name until just now."

"Okay," nodded Mrs. Gorman. "She is…She will be…one hundred and four next week."

Andy couldn't even imagine living past thirty, much less past one hundred.

"Oh…" was all he could say.

"Some people…" began Mrs. Gorman.

She shuddered a little and held both of her arms for a second before continuing on.

Andy did not know what to make of that little affect, but he listened intently. Something strange was going on with his landlady, and he wanted to find out what that could possibly be.

"Some people live past their time," nodded Mrs. Gorman. "I think…no, I believe…there are two reasons this can happen. Some people live past their time because of love. They love life, they love others, and they're loved by others, and that's fine. I think God allows this as a reward for good people…but some people…some people live past their time out of sheer hate…just sheer, unadulterated hate."

"*Oooh*…uhhh…" said Andy.

Yeah, he had no idea where this was going.

"You see, some people just hate everything," nodded Mrs. Gorman as she frowned at the same time. "They just hate the world and everything in it, but they're also afraid of dying, so they use that hatred, that *power*, to just keep right on going."

"I…see…" said Andy uncomfortably.

This was getting weird.

"That woman upstairs is the meanest ball of hate I have ever had the unfortunate occurrence to meet," frowned Mrs. Gorman.

This, of course, didn't make a whole lot of sense to Andy. Mrs. Gorman was the landlady, after all. She didn't have to rent to Mrs. Arkle. She could just pick and choose her renters.

"So why do you rent to her?" asked Andy. "I don't understand."

"She came with the building," shrugged the older woman. "It was in the contract when my late husband bought the place. Can't kick her out, and she has nowhere else to go anyway, and even though she may be…ugh…I'm still Christian enough to take her money."

"Oh…Okay," said Andy uncertainly. "What does this have to do with me?"

"Just don't interact with her at all," warned Mrs. Gorman as she waved her hands flat, palms down, in front of herself. "Not at *all*."

"Uhhh…noted," nodded Andy.

"You see…" said the older woman in a cautious tone. "You…You have to understand. We have delivery people that come by and drop groceries and goods off to her, and she has a personal caretaker that comes by every day in the morning. Her caretakers switch out, and they leave around this time of day, but…I just…I would not interact with her at all. In fact, I feel sorry for those people who do have to work with her. I, personally, wouldn't deal with her at all if it weren't necessary."

"Got it," nodded Andy again.

"Some people think they can outsmart death," frowned Mrs. Gorman as she shook her head for visible emphasis. "We both know you can't do that…but even worse…some people think they can outsmart *Hell*.

"That woman upstairs was married three times, and she lost all three husbands under suspicious circumstances. All of her kids are dead, too. All three of them died when they were little, also under strange circumstances. I'd say she's cursed, but I don't believe in curses. I believe in God Almighty, and I'll tell you what…I don't trust that woman as far as I can throw her."

"Oof," said Andy with wide eyes.

He didn't like the sound of that. Of course, what could a one-hundred-and-four-year-old woman do to him? There was no reason to be scared of the old biddy.

"You just keep to yourself, and you'll be fine," nodded Mrs. Gorman.

"Will do," nodded Andy in return.

"Well, I should be going," said the older woman. "I'll let you get back to settling in, but if you have any questions, you have my number. You're paid up in full for six months, and I really appreciate the forward pay. There aren't a lot of folks who can afford to do that in this economy."

"Absolutely," nodded Andy. "You are most welcome."

He said his goodbyes to the older woman after that, and she left without further gossip. This was a good thing, of course, because it was time to get back to his beer, and more importantly, to the game.

He sat down in his recliner, grabbed his beer, and had taken one sip just before the doorbell rang again.

"What the…?" he said in exasperation.

He set down his beer, walked to the front door, and answered the door for whomever this new caller was going to be.

An older man with white hair, someone at least in his seventies, stood before Andy. This man was dressed in overalls and a brown T-shirt, though his presence here was a mystery.

"Andy?" asked the older man.

"Uhhhh…yeah," replied Andy.

The old man held out his right hand, and Andy shook it out of courtesy.

"I'm Gerald," nodded the old man. "I fix things around the building."

"Oh…" said Andy in swift comprehension.

It made sense. This guy was the handyman or something.

"Can I help you?" asked Andy.

"I just need to go over a few things with you, and then I'll be on my way," nodded Gerald.

"Gotcha," nodded Andy.

The old man walked in without being invited, just like Mrs. Gorman had.

"I'll be out of your hair in a jiffy," said the old man. "Let me just explain a few things."

"Okay," replied Andy.

"Now this building is old, but it's also unique," said the handyman. "It has some features that other buildings don't have. Here, let me show you."

He walked past Andy and led them both toward the kitchen. They walked through the living room and into the kitchen, though Andy stared longingly at his game and his beer for a few seconds before entering the kitchen after the old man.

"Now this is a fairly big kitchen compared to other apartments," explained Gerald. "That's because this place was originally a two-story house, so what we have here is a converted lower floor."

"Gotcha," said Andy.

"Over by these cabinets…if you look here…" pointed the old man.

Andy looked over toward the east side of the kitchen where there were some cabinets and a countertop with a set of drawers underneath it. The old handyman directed Andy's attention toward what looked like an old-fashioned intercom that rested upon the white wall in-between the countertop and the cabinets above.

The old intercom was a big brown block of painted metal with the waffled circle of a black speaker upon it, a large red push button underneath said speaker. It looked seriously dated, like something out of the '40s or '50s, maybe.

"We have this speaker in here because it's part of the building ownership clause," said Gerald matter-of-factly. "In other words, it came with the building, and we can't remove it. All I can do is repair it."

"Okay," nodded Andy. "What's it do?"

The old man's wrinkled face darkened for a quick second, but then he continued speaking as if everything was fine, though Andy had caught that change in mood, short as it had been.

"It connects with the one upstairs," said Gerald. "Mrs. Arkle has one, but I seriously doubt she'll ever use hers, so you should *never…ever…*mess around with this. I'd like to get rid of it, but it's part of the building's ownership clause, so all I can do is fix it."

"Okay…" said Andy uncertainly.

"If you have friends over, they shouldn't mess with it, either," warned Gerald.

"Got it," nodded Andy.

"Now, this place is old and has its quirks, so you may have trouble with the heating and cooling," explained the old handyman. "If that happens, you just call me. Don't try and fix it yourself, and don't hire someone else to do it. You'll violate your lease."

"Okay," said Andy.

"Yeah, this building is definitely unique," said the old man. "There are some interesting secrets here and there, but don't go messing with anything. For example, there's actually an old dumbwaiter that was sealed up here in this back wall."

He led Andy through the back kitchen door into the tiny laundry area. The old handyman pointed toward a blank white wall, and Andy could make out the indented shape of a pseudo-door, a rectangle about half-the-size of a person, though that rectangle was painted over in said white.

"As long as you don't try and do any renovations yourself, you're fine," explained the old man. "Just remember to call me if anything goes wrong. Mrs. Gorman can't violate any of the building ownership clauses without a serious fine, and she could even lose the property over a violation."

"Got it," nodded Andy.

"My number's on the fridge," said Gerald. "You just give me a holler when you need me."

"Will do," said Andy.

They walked back through the kitchen and back out into the living room. The old man said his goodbyes and left, and Andy breathed out a long-overdue sigh of relief.

"Finally…" he muttered.

It was game time.

He sat down in his comfy chair, reached over for his remote, and turned up the volume on his TV. He took one sip of his beer and nearly spit it out as the doorbell rang yet again.

"Oh, come on!" he said angrily.

Okay, now he was getting mad.

He slammed the open palms of his hands down upon the arms of his chair, stood up, and stormed over to the front door.

"Do I even get to enjoy my own place!" he said angrily.

Andy opened the front door, but there was no one there. There was a cardboard box in a person's place, an inconspicuous package that had just arrived via the mail, though the timing on its delivery was impeccably terrible.

"I don't remember ordering anything," he muttered as he picked up the package and shut the door in an absent-minded fashion.

The package was indeed addressed to him, but try as he might, he could not remember ordering anything at all. Plus, he had just fully moved in today.

There was no return-to-sender label.

"Huh…" he said warily.

He took the small box into the kitchen, set the package down upon the kitchen-sink counter, and opened up a drawer in which he had stashed a few pieces of silverware. He pulled out a serrated kitchen knife and sawed through the tape that was holding shut the unexpected delivery. He opened up the box, stared down at its contents, and pulled forth the article of clothing contained within.

At first, he did not know what he was looking at.

"What is this?" breathed Andy.

He spread out the black cloth and studied it a bit before he understood what it was he had in his hands. He held out a black shawl made of knit wool, something he would have never ordered on his own.

"You've got to be kidding me!" he laughed.

He took the article of clothing back into the living room and draped it over his shoulders. It smelled okay, and it was a little added comfort to his game time. Besides, he'd deal with it later. Someone had obviously sent this to him by mistake, but maybe his girlfriend would like it, so there was that.

"Game time," he said to himself as he sat back down in his chair.

He leaned back, adjusted the black shawl around his shoulders, picked up his beer, and smiled as he finally got to enjoy his game.

✳✳✳✳✳

Andy snapped awake with a snort. He had a mild hangover, but he was used to that.

"Price you pay for a few beers," he said to himself.

He sat up in his chair, let the black shawl around his shoulders slip off him, and stood up. His mouth was dry, his throat parched, so it was time for some water, maybe some soda.

He breathed out a wisp of steam as his breath crystallized in the cold air around him. It took him a moment to figure out that the whole place was freezing.

"What the…?" he muttered to himself.

He walked over to the east wall where the bathroom was located. That was also where the thermostat was, so he took a quick peek at it.

"Twenty-seven degrees?" said Andy in disbelief. "What in the blue blazes?"

The thermostat was clearly very old, a model he couldn't even begin to recognize. It wasn't even electronic, though he was sure that couldn't affect the AC, not this much. The black needle on the number line already indicated that the thermostat was turned up to a comfortable seventy-two degrees, but the red needle, the one for the actual temperature, was on twenty-seven, so there wasn't much he could do anyway.

"Of course," he breathed out. "Time to call…uhhh…Gerald."

He walked back to his comfy chair and picked up his phone. He picked up the large rectangle and hit the side button to bring up the screen, but nothing happened.

"Naturally!" he said angrily.

He walked into the kitchen in order to plug in his phone. That's where he'd left his charger.

He placed his phone on the kitchen counter, plugged it in, and walked back out to the living room. It was too cold in here, so stepping outside for a moment would help. It was hot as heck out there right now. In fact, being the height of summer, it was in the nineties outside.

"I'll just step out for a moment," he said as he rubbed his arms for warmth.

He walked to the front door and turned the knob, but the metal was cold, so cold that he nearly let go of it. Not that it mattered…The door would not budge.

"What!" he hissed.

He rattled the door and pulled hard on it, but he had to let go of the knob due to the sheer lack of heat that was counterintuitively burning his hand.

Andy swore as he shook his right hand to put back some warmth into it.

His breath was coming out in large streams of steam now, the air crystalizing in a line as if he were smoking.

"This is some bull…" he muttered, but he did not finish that expletive.

He rubbed his arms for warmth, spied the black shawl upon his comfy chair, walked back to his chair, and immediately snatched up the article of clothing. He draped the shawl around the top of his sports shirt before rubbing his palms together to generate some friction. He breathed on his hands and then thought better about his situation.

"Good thing I made the bed," he said as he shivered. "Just grab a blanket real fast…"

He walked to his bedroom door over on the west side of his new place, opened the door, and stepped into his bedroom. A quick glance at the clock told him it was only six, well before nightfall, so light was still streaming in through the windows.

"Yeah, I'll get out through the window," he said to himself.

He walked to the bedroom window in order to open it, but there was no latch or way to raise the thing. His bedroom window was simply a crossing of rectangular wood latticed over small panes of glass, the whole of it sealed into the foundation.

"What the fu…?" he started to swear.

He felt a cold presence behind him, a black omen of sorts, something he could not explain with mere words.

Andy turned and then stood as still as a statue as he viewed his bed. The dark-blue comforter upon the bed was raised up as if someone were beneath it, as if someone were kneeling upon his bed, draped by his bedspread so that they could not be seen.

He leaned against the window in startled surprise, but he did not cry out. He was no coward, but if there was a stranger in his place, he was going to deal with them right here and now.

He reached over to where he had his wooden baseball bat. He had leaned it against his oak dresser, so he picked up the makeshift weapon with the full intent of using it when necessary.

He edged closer to his bed in cautious steps, raising his bat, ready to deal with this threat the old-fashioned way. He reached forward toward the edge of his bedspread with his left hand, gripped the edge of his dark-blue comforter, and pulled hard on the spread. He whipped off the blanket from the bed and immediately gripped his bat with both hands, prepared to swing.

There was nothing underneath the blanket.

He breathed out a sigh of relief. It occurred to him that his idiot friends had propped up the comforter somehow in order to scare him.

"Those jerks," he chuckled. "Oh, it is on n—"

His sentence died in his throat as he heard a giggling behind him, a higher-pitched laughter as one would hear from a child. He whipped around to catch the image of that child, a little towheaded boy dressed in brown Sunday-school clothes, that boy just outside the doorframe of his bedroom.

The boy disappeared as he darted away from the door and out of Andy's field of vision.

"Hey!" yelled Andy.

He dropped his bat and gave chase by running out his bedroom door, but there was no sign of the kid in the living room, and even looking over into the kitchen revealed nothing.

The fine hairs on the back of his neck stood on end. Something very strange was going on, something very wrong, and he wanted no part of it.

He walked back into his bedroom, grabbed his comforter, and wrapped the dark-blue blanket around his shoulders to add to the protection the black shawl was already giving him. It was cold as heck in here, and for some ungodly reason, he was trapped within his own apartment.

His breath came out in large puffs of steam as he made his way over to his thermostat again. One check of the red needle revealed the little crimson arrow to be centered over the zero.

"Z...z...zero!" he said through chattering teeth. "I gotta get outta here!"

He walked to the front door, but he stopped as he studied the main entrance and exit to his new place of residence. The door was now coated over with ivory-white hoarfrost, like the back of a freezer that hadn't been defrosted in ages.

"Un...b...b...believable," he chattered out.

His phone had to have charged by now. It had to have some charge in it. He just needed enough juice to get Gerald over here to rescue him. Besides, that kid was still wandering around his place. That couldn't have been his imagination. That little boy was still hiding in here somewhere.

He walked into the kitchen and went for his phone, but as he tried to pick it up, he realized it was stuck to the countertop. Correction: It was *frozen* to the countertop.

"You have got to be kidding me!" yelled Andy.

His phone was as cold as a slab of ice, and bending down revealed to him that the bottom edges were frosted over like the front door.

He hit the side button to bring up the screen, but once again, nothing happened.

"Come on!" he hissed.

He walked over to his silverware drawer, pulled it open, and took out the first knife his fingers made contact with. It was his good silver butterknife, the one his Aunt Margaret had given him way, way back when.

He really didn't want to use his best piece of silverware to pry his phone from the countertop, but he also didn't want to freeze to death in his new apartment when it was the hottest day of the year outside, a fate that would be an irony for the ages. Besides, he was all out of patience.

"Decisions, decisions," he breathed out. "You know what?...Screw it."

He turned around to get back to the task at hand, but he received yet another start, this one a lot more alarming than the previous two, much more alarming than the boy and the bedsheet.

There was a man standing in his kitchen.

There was a balding man in a brown smoking jacket and good brown slacks standing in the middle of his kitchen. This guy looked to be in his early thirties, and he was standing to where Andy could only see his right profile, the man staring off toward the laundry room, staring away as if at nothing. In his right hand was a half-consumed dirty martini, the olives on a stick still balanced on the side of the fanned glass.

"Umm…uhhh…can I help you?" asked Andy.

He was truly at a loss for words over this one.

The stranger slowly turned to look at him, but Andy immediately regretted that he had.

The left half of this man's clothes were charred rags, but it was his neck and face that really showed the damage. The stranger's neck and face were horribly burned, but not in an old, scarred way, but fresh, as if the fire had just been put out. His left hand was also charred and blackened, fresh blood seeping from the lines of burnt flesh upon it.

Andy's mouth dropped open as he clutched the poor weapon that was his Aunt Margaret's silver butterknife. He could do nothing but gasp out a stream of crystallized breath at the sight of this horror, for he was frozen at that moment, and not from the invasive cold around him.

The stranger turned and walked toward the laundry room, disappearing a moment later through the open doorway.

Andy cautiously followed him to the laundry room doorway and slowly peered through the opening and into the sliver of room that made up his laundry area.

There was no one there.

There was, however, the backdoor, the backdoor that led out into the tiny backyard of this property, the backdoor that he had clearly forgotten about until now.

"Y…Y…Yes!" said Andy through chattering teeth.

It was time to get out of this horror show and time to get out of this lease. Whatever was going on here was beyond his understanding, so it was better to just cut and run now.

He walked past the washer and dryer to reach for the brass knob, but that knob was frosted over just like the front door. Andy braved the absolute chill of the metal, but try as he might, he could not open the door. It was stuck shut, frozen shut, just like the front door.

He let off a string of expletives that would have made a sailor proud.

He pulled his comforter closer to him and shivered beneath it. Something had to be done, and it had to be done now, because this was getting ridiculous.

He walked back into the kitchen and spied the old intercom out of his right peripheral. He wasn't supposed to use it, but it occurred to him that the old woman upstairs might be able to contact someone. She probably had one of those alert systems that old people needed in case they fell or something.

He walked over to the intercom, and thankfully, it wasn't frosted over. He pushed the big red button on it, held it in, and leaned in to speak into the archaic device.

"H…Hello?" he stammered. "Is anybody there? Mrs. Arkle?"

He released the button and waited, but there was no reply, just a mild static noise of the old intercom working to its, what he assumed, full capacity.

"Hello?" he asked again. "Mrs. Arkle? Are you there? I need help."

He released the button again, but this time a voice floated through over the speaker.

"Yes?" came an old woman's voice.

Andy grinned in spite of himself. Now he could get some help. He could get out of this freakshow of an apartment.

He pushed in the button in order to talk.

"This is Andy Warnell," he replied. "I'm your downstairs neighbor."

"I know who you are, Mr. Warnell," said the old woman in return.

Mrs. Arkle's voice was raspy but understandable. Even so, there was a touch of irritation in her tone, a spark of something Andy did not like. Nevertheless, he decided to play it safe and just ask for help.

"There's something wrong with the A.C. down here," he said. "Everything's frozen over, and I can't get out the doors. They're frozen shut. Even my phone won't work."

"And?" asked the old woman.

That was not the response Andy had expected to hear.

"And I need help," he continued. "Please, call someone…uhhh…Gerald to come over and let me out. I don't want to have to smash a window or something."

"Damaging the property will violate your lease, Mr. Warnell," replied Mrs. Arkle.

"I'm leaving anyway," said Andy. "I don't think this place is right for me…Could you please contact Gerald?"

"I'm afraid I can't do that, Mr. Warnell," said the old woman.

"Wait, what?" asked Andy.

He wasn't sure he'd heard right.

"It's quite warm up here," continued the old woman. "It's exactly the temperature I need. I don't want you fooling around with the heating and cooling. If you're too cold, cover up with something. I'm sure there's something lying around that you can wear."

"I…No, wait. You don't under—" began Andy.

"Good day, Mr. Warnell," said the old woman. "Don't contact me again."

"Wait, I…" started Andy, but then he stepped back out of frustration.

He let out another long string of curses. It took him a few seconds to calm down after that, but he managed it.

"That woman is mean," he grimaced. "Okay, okay. Think…"

He remembered watching a movie about a guy who had messed around with an old thermostat and had gotten it to work. That guy had taken off the thermostat's cover and had messed around with a small vial of mercury set within the guts of the thing.

"That's what I'll d…do…" said Andy through chattering teeth.

He switched his butterknife to his left hand, pulled his comforter tightly to him, and walked back into the living room, intent on fixing the thermostat. He walked to the east wall where the thermostat was located and gingerly reached up for it.

The paneled dark wood of the wall beneath the thermostat broke open, and Andy cried out as he stepped backwards in alarm. Something had popped out of the wall as if shoved through it, and it took Andy a moment to figure out what he was looking at.

It was a little girl, or at least, what was left of one.

The little girl before him was half-in and half-out of the wall, and she looked to have been around five or six. She wore a blue dress with red-flower print, but she had been dead for many, many years, a withered mummy of a thing with wisps of strawberry-blonde hair upon her shriveled skull.

"Oh…Oh…Oh, sh…shi…" stammered out Andy.

He just had fear in him. No thoughts, no answers, no anything but fear.

In the little girl's withered right arm was a tattered teddy bear, and in her left hand, the arm dangling down as if weighted in place, was some kind of black book, what looked to be an old album of sorts, but Andy couldn't tell for sure.

"What?...What is…is going on?" he asked himself.

He was still in shock, but necessity overrode that little issue. He still needed to fix the thermostat. He could call the police about the body once he'd escaped from this nightmare prison he'd somehow been roped into, and the only way he was going to escape was to thaw the place out.

He reached up to fix the thermostat, intent on removing the casing. He had shut off part of his brain in order to do this, because just below him was the body of the little girl, and he did not want to look at it, much less think about it.

His fingers touched the plastic casing of the thermostat, but he did not get to remove the protective cover.

The girl beneath him turned her shriveled skull of a face up toward him, her jaws creaking open, and she hissed out a dry screech that pierced Andy's hearing.

That was it for him. He backed away and ran toward the kitchen. There was no going out the front door anyway.

Andy ran into the kitchen and immediately jammed his thumb into the red button on the old intercom.

"Mrs. Arkle! Mrs. Arkle!" he called out.

There was a moment of static, and then he received his reply.

"Mr. Warnell, I thought I told you not to contact me again," came the old woman's raspy voice.

"Th…There's a body in the wall!" stammered Andy.

"Excuse me?" asked Mrs. Arkle.

"A b…body in the wall!" repeated Andy. "I saw it! It was a little girl with a teddy bear."

"Is that so?" asked the old woman. "You are unhinged, Mr. Warnell. I will have to take this up with Mrs. Gorman as soon as possible."

"N…No!" chattered Andy. "There's a dead little girl in the wall, and she…she screamed at me."

He realized right then that he was sounding like a crazy person, a real loon, and he needed to get a grip, if only to convince this pernicious old bat to help him.

"This conversation is over, Mr. Warnell," said Mrs. Arkle.

"L…Look, just c…call Mrs. Gorman and get Gerald t…t…to come over here," said Andy through chattering teeth.

"I'll inform them tomorrow," said Mrs. Arkle. "I'll be sure to raise a serious complaint over this."

"N…No, it's too cold!" hissed Andy. "Get them now! I'm t…trapped in here!"

"The temperature is just fine up here, Mr. Warnell," said the old woman. "There are no dead bodies here either, but I'll be sure and inform the police about yours tomorrow. Right now, I'm going to enjoy some chamomile. Good day, Mr. Warnell."

"Y…You old bat!" yelled Andy.

He gave up on that for now. Maybe if he enraged her enough, she'd call the police, and that would actually be a good thing, but for now, he needed heat.

"Th…The stove…" he said to himself.

He hadn't tried turning on the oven. Even the burners up top would help.

He walked over to the stove but was supremely disappointed at what he saw. The burners on top were electric, so that meant no immediate heat, but he could always turn on the actual oven.

There were no dials on the oven…It was all electronic. The clock on the stove was not working, either. There was just a blank black bar where the time should have been.

He jammed his thumb into the flat buttons for the temperature, but nothing happened. It was clear the power was dead.

"No, no, no, no, NO!" yelled Andy.

This was way past ridiculous. He needed to get out of this frozen hellhole, and fast.

"No wonder this place was s…so ch…cheap," he said as he shivered uncontrollably.

He turned around and stopped as yet another stranger walked through his kitchen. This time it was a young man, a young black-haired man in his late twenties, that man wearing a simple brown overcoat with black pants.

Andy realized he was still clutching his silver butterknife. He switched it to his right hand, ready to bring it up just in case.

The man walking through his kitchen had his left profile facing Andy, as if the intruder had come from out of the laundry room. This young man stopped and turned to give a brief stare at Andy, but once again, Andy severely wished that this new stranger had not done so, just like the last intruder in his kitchen.

Half the stranger's head was missing, the right half, just a chunk gone, like he'd been the victim of a shotgun blast, probably, but Andy was no forensics expert.

The macabre intruder turned his head back to stare at nothing, walked out of the kitchen, turned left, and entered Andy's bedroom.

"Y…Yep," chattered Andy. "Yep. Yep, yep. Another one. Another one f…for crazy town."

There was no point in explaining it. He was just taking this crap as fact now.

He pulled his comforter closer to him. It had to be way below zero in here now. One glance around the kitchen told him that anyway; almost everything was coated over with white hoarfrost, some of it forming into thick chunks of snow-covered ice.

He heard the crying of a baby a second later, a loud wailing as if an infant were in pain or danger.

"Oh…Oh, crap…" he said to himself.

This one he could not ignore.

He walked out into the living room and looked around for the source of the crying, but his ears were a better cue than any visual one. That wailing was coming from his bathroom.

He walked into the bathroom and searched for the source of his distress. The wailing was intense upon entering, and it was coming from the bathtub, so he pulled back the ugly green shower curtain that had come with the place and stared down into the contents of the tub.

He could see the baby under the ice. The tub was half-filled with water, that water frozen solid, and he could see the bluish skin and little light-blue onesie of a baby in that block of death, but he backed away from that terrible vision. This one he couldn't really handle.

He sucked in his breath as he backed out of the bathroom. He reached forward and pulled the door closed, but not all the way. The doorknob was frozen solid, a cold chunk of metal, and it burned to the touch. Nevertheless, he wanted the terrible image from the tub out of his field of vision.

The little girl was one thing, but the frozen baby was entirely another. Either he was going crazy because of the cold, or this place…this place was…

"Th…This place is haunted as fu—" he began to swear, but he didn't get the chance to finish that sentence.

The door creaked open a little, more than enough to stop his current assessment of his unfortunate situation.

He could see through the open slat of the bathroom door, and a man, a big man, a man that looked to be in his late thirties, came crawling into Andy's field of vision, right from the area Andy had just left.

This guy was dressed in light-blue work overalls, the kind a mechanic might have. He had shaggy brown hair, a full brown beard and mustache, and his rugged face was wracked with pain. Andy could see the guy dragging a pair of crushed legs behind him, leaving a trail of blood upon the white of the bathroom tiles, that trail coming out and over the lip of the tub, as if he'd just crawled out of it. The man's tortured expression was further enhanced by the blood seeping from his lips, a sure sign that he had internal injuries as well.

Andy shut the bathroom door all the way. He wasn't going to deal with that.

He turned and let out a small cry of surprise at the sight of the little boy standing in front of him, the little blond boy he'd seen earlier.

This kid held up a cardboard box of what looked like chocolates and asked Andy a simple question.

"Want some candy?" asked the boy.

"Uhhh…" began Andy.

The boy smiled, and blood immediately spilled in a river from his thin lips, running down his chin and onto his good Sunday clothes.

Enough was enough. Andy was way past his limit.

He walked past the kid and into the kitchen. Things were way out of control now. Whatever was going on here was way out of his paygrade, and he needed some answers.

He switched his silver butterknife to his left hand and jammed his right thumb into the big red button of the intercom.

"What's going on…d…down here, Mrs. Arkle?" he asked.

He waited a bit, and sure enough, the old bat answered.

"Whatever could you mean, Mr. Warnell?" asked Mrs. Arkle.

"The place has…has t…t…turned into Antarctica," chattered Andy. "Oh…Oh, yeah, and…and one more thing…There are *dead* people wandering around in…in here."

"Is that right, Mr. Warnell?" asked the old woman. "Are you finished?"

"N…Not by a longshot," replied Andy. "G…Get the police over here."

"I don't think so, Mr. Warnell," said Mrs. Arkle. "My suggestion is to stop drinking or doing the drugs you young people like to do. I'm doing you a favor by not calling anyone. That way, you can't be taken to jail."

"A f…f…favor, huh?" asked Andy. "You w…want to do me a favor, then c…call somebody over here to let me out! I'm freezing to death in my own home!"

"It's not your home, Mr. Warnell," stated Mrs. Arkle. "It's mine. You are fortunate to be renting here. As for freezing to death, perhaps it's just your time…You know, this must mean you're not a Christian man, Mr. Warnell. Most people think Hell is a place of fire and brimstone, but I know it to be cold."

"What?" asked Andy in confusion.

"It looks like your time is running out, Mr. Warnell," said the old woman. "My guess is the Devil has come for you."

"Y…You old bat!" yelled Andy.

"It's the chill of death, Mr. Warnell," said Mrs. Arkle, a hint of amusement in her raspy voice. "It looks like your fate has already been decided. Where you're going, there is no light. There's only darkness, darkness and cold. That's right, Mr. Warnell. It's just bitter, bitter cold you're heading for."

"You…so help me…I'll…I will—" stammered Andy.

"Farewell, Mr. Warnell," said the old woman. "I doubt we shall speak again, in this life or the next. I'm afraid we'll be a great distance apart. Where I'm going is warm."

The intercom went dead as Andy watched a coating of frost spread across it, spreading across the archaic device in real time, something unbelievable if he hadn't been staring straight at it.

"You p…p…piece of…" he half-cursed.

He shook his head in disgust and marched back into the living room. He was truly angry now, so some dead people were not going to stop him from getting out of this frozen hell, and Hell it was, the one and only thing the old bat upstairs had been correct about.

Andy turned and stared at the supposedly dead girl still hanging half-out of his wall underneath the thermostat. He stared at the black book in her withered, dangling left hand, the book that looked like a photo album, and he decided then and there to get it. Maybe it held some answers, at least, these things always held answers in the movies. Some kind of unfinished business or some such crap.

He walked up to the small corpse and reached for the book, but the girl's shriveled skull of a head peered up at him with empty sockets and hissed at him through grinning teeth.

"Oh, shut up," said Andy.

He was still holding his Aunt Margaret's silver butterknife in his left hand. He really didn't want to touch this thing residing in his wall, so he placed the flat of the blade against the dead leathery skin of her forehead, ready to push her head back so those teeth could not bite him.

It did not work as intended. The dead girl's skull sizzled and popped under the touch of the knife, and she shrieked in terrible anguish as Andy yanked the black photo album from her withered, skeletal left hand.

"Y…Yeah, how do you like that! Who's got game now, huh!" he yelled, but then he stopped as he realized the insanity of his action.

He was yelling at a corpse, an animated one, true, but still. He thought better about his situation now anyway.

"S…Silver," he said. "At…At least that works."

The shriveled and withered corpse of the little girl slumped over and went back to playing dead.

Good enough for him.

He shook his head and backed away with his new prize. He opened the old photo album and flipped through it one page at a time.

There were a lot of black and white photos within the book, but the age of the pictures was not what stoked his interest. It was the people in the photos that held his focus.

He saw the faces of the dead within this album, the boy, the girl, all three men, even the baby…but one of those faces he had not seen before. The same woman was in each and every picture, a woman with light hair, probably blonde, a woman whose presence had not shown as of yet in his apartment.

There was cursive writing penned under a few of the photos, a rare occurrence, three to be exact, but he studied those words with new gusto.

"Peter F…Feldman and family, 1945," he whispered under chilled breath.

There was a picture of the young man who he'd seen with half a head missing. There was also the unknown blonde woman and the baby, the woman holding the baby in both arms. The man in the picture, this Peter Feldman, held a shotgun in his right hand, the firearm leaning against his right shoulder. He had a dead turkey held up by the legs in his left hand.

"Looks like you w…were on the wrong end of th…that shot, bud," said Andy.

He flipped to the next photo with writing and studied that picture's caption.

"D…Doctor Eric Edelman and family, 1951," he whispered again.

This picture was of the balding man in the smoking jacket. Next to him was the unknown blonde and the little blonde boy. Andy could clearly see a barbecue grill to their right, and the woman in the picture held a small metal can of what looked like charcoal lighter fluid.

"I c…can only guess what happened th…there," he chattered out.

Andy flipped through until he found the last picture with a caption.

"J…Jack Glover and family, 1957," he said.

It was the big man he'd seen with the crushed legs. This man was standing in front of an old car, the little girl next to him, her right arm clutching her teddy bear tightly to her. The unknown blonde woman stood on the left side of the little girl, the right side from Andy's point of view. The man was dressed in the same overalls that had been showcased during his grisly appearance, only this time with a toolbelt around his waist. Andy could see that the car behind the family was lifted up on a large metal pump jack, the tires missing from the vehicle itself.

The next few photos held no captions, but they did hold something of extreme interest. They were of the unknown blonde woman, singular, just still images of her by her lonesome, but that was not interesting. It was the black shawl around the woman's shoulders that caught his eye, the very shawl he was wearing right now, right now around his own shoulders underneath his comforter.

He flipped to the back of the book and felt his blood boil at the name penned upon the last white page. It was actually this name at the back of the book that set him off and really got his goat.

"Property of Maxine Arkle, huh!" he spat.

It hit him like a bolt of lightning, all of it, all of it at once.

He knew what was going on now. He knew what was going on, and he had an idea of how to stop it. It was the bottom of the ninth, and the bases were loaded…He just needed that grand slam.

"Th…Think you can…can outsmart Hell, do you!" he asked. "Using me as a…as a patsy, huh!"

Andy pitched the book to the floor, walked into his bedroom, and grabbed his baseball bat. It was time to hit that grand slam.

"You are d…done, Grandma!" he spat. "Murder your own family and want me to…to…t…take the fall! No, no…N…Not today, you old bat. Not any day!"

He walked out of his bedroom and stopped to view the empty hole in his wall. The little dead girl was gone, a vacant space where she had just been.

"Wonderful," he said unhappily.

He walked into his kitchen in order to head to the laundry room, but he was stopped yet again by the crowd before him.

They were all there, the faces of the dead from the album, all of them in their own grisly glory, even the withered little wall girl holding the frozen baby, all of them waiting to bar his way.

He had his bat, and he had his knife, and he could possibly fight his way through, but he had a better idea, something he had not tried as of yet.

Andy slowly placed his silver knife on the east wall countertop, reached up inside his comforter, and pulled off the black shawl. He held up the cursed article of clothing and showed it off as if it were the grand prize of a gameshow.

"It's n…not me," he chattered out. "It's not me y…you want. You just s…step aside, and I'll lead the way. I'll t…take you to her."

He held up the black shawl and marched forward, the ghosts of the past parting for him as he made his way through them. He stepped into the laundry room, let his comforter slide from his shoulders, wrapped the black shawl back around him, gripped his wooden bat, and swung hard at the east wall.

The plaster came apart, the thin wooden panel behind it breaking as he smashed into it, knocking forth a hole to reveal the rectangular space he was looking for. He pulled chunks of frozen plaster from the wall until there was just enough space to crawl into the old, unused dumbwaiter.

The dumbwaiter was set aways back from the wall, a clear indication this old building had been remodeled who knew how many times. The old rope that worked this device dangled in front of it, so he pushed that rope aside for obvious reasons.

He climbed into the old service device and pulled hard on the cold, thick rope that pulled this thing up. It was a tough pull to get his own weight moving, but he would smash through the top of the dumbwaiter and climb that rope if need be.

"I'm c…coming for you, you old bat," he said angrily.

There was no light in here, just pitch black, but he knew he was going up. He was going up and out of this cold darkness, and he was going to make sure that evil old woman took his place.

He pulled his way up to the second floor, pulling hard until the dumbwaiter could no longer move. He pulled on the rope with all of his weight to hold the device in place, and then he kicked forth at the plaster he instinctively knew was right in front of him. His tennis shoes blasted through that weak wall, and then light spilled in.

He burst from the hole and into heat, wonderful and glorious heat.

Andy stood up in a small laundry area reminiscent of his own. Light was spilling into this room from the open archway that led into the kitchen area, no door to shut for this particular covey.

He walked into this new kitchen and dropped his wooden bat to have it clatter across the kitchen floor. He didn't need it anymore, not for this.

He pulled off the black shawl and gripped the cursed article of clothing in his right hand.

He walked into the living room and spied her there, the old woman sitting in a wheelchair, the old bat just sitting there as if nothing were wrong.

She was older than dirt, a wrinkled thing of frowns and hate dressed in black, a monochrome of evil that he had the cure for.

She looked up and saw him walk in, the light in her once bright-blue eyes flashing a silent fury, a recognition that her time was finally up. She lifted her wrinkled, liver-spotted right hand, lifted it a mere inch as if under great strain, and pointed at him with one accusing finger.

"You…aren't…welcome…here…Mister…Warnell…" she said in raspy, measured breaths.

How in the heck she had operated the intercom so quickly was beyond Andy, because this woman could barely move or talk at all, but that was beside the point, because none of this had been right from the get go. He just took it all as fact now. If it was hate that was keeping her going, then it didn't surprise him at all that she had somehow used that intercom, had somehow brought forth some evil power to use against him.

But that was irrelevant. Her time was up.

"I just stopped by for a little 'wellness check,'" smirked Andy. "Just being neighborly."

"Go…to…He—" started Mrs. Arkle, but Andy cut her short.

"Oh, I won't be the one going there," he said firmly.

He held up the black shawl, the black shawl he knew to be hers, the fetter that brought in the cold of Hell and the ghosts from the past, and she visibly recoiled from it. That was all the proof he needed to seal her fate. She couldn't outsmart death this time, and he was going to make damned sure she didn't outsmart Hell.

"You see, there's a draft in your laundry room," he smiled. "It's going to get chilly, so I came up to return this to you. We don't want you to get cold, now do we?"

He draped the heavy shawl around the old woman's shoulders and walked to her front door, but not before giving her one last backwards glance.

He could already feel the chill settling in here. It was a blanket of cold coming down, a Shakespearian revenge that was best served as such.

"Goodbye, Mrs. Arkle," he said firmly. "I doubt we'll meet again in this lifetime or the next. You've got a cold front coming in, but I'm actually going somewhere warm. Oh, but I wouldn't worry, because you won't be lonely. You have family stopping by. I imagine they'll be here sooner than later."

"This…isn't…over…" rasped out Mrs. Arkle.

"Oh, it is for me, Mrs. Arkle," replied Andy. "It is for me…Say hi to the kids for me."

Andy opened the front door and stepped out into the summer heat. Yeah, it was sweltering outside, but he breathed in that heat with gusto, reveling in that hot air as he stood for a moment on the second-floor stairs.

He smiled, reached back, and shut the door behind him.

#10…BREATHE

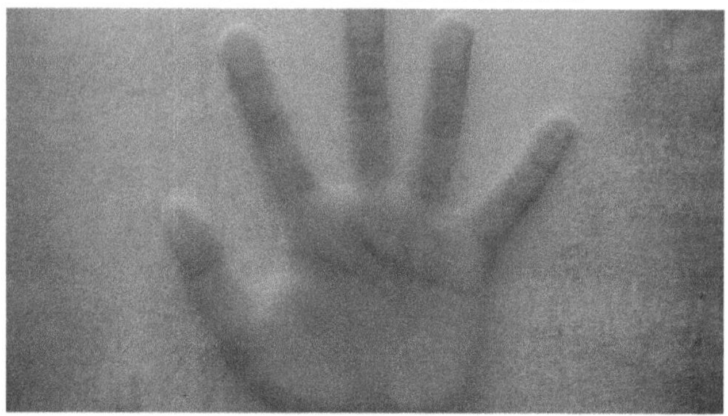

How long can you hold your breath?

Scott walked along the edge of Prisoner's Creek, his best friend, Danny, right behind him. It was a hot summer Sunday, and the bugs were out, but there was nothing else to do, so it was either this or going back home to play with the ball and glove. Church was out, and they'd already watched the latest episode of *Sky King,* so what else was there to do?

Scott was twelve, and Danny had just turned twelve, so they were two peas in a pod, best friends since they were eight and seven respectively, and Prisoner's Creek was their latest hangout.

Prisoner's Creek was too wide and too fast to be an actual creek, but it was also too small to be a river, but that didn't matter to the locals. It was considered a bad fishing spot, and it had a bad reputation, but Scott wasn't scared of coming down here. No one ever came down here, which made it perfect for he and Danny to use as their own private sanctuary, a place to escape the sulk and boredom of small-town life.

Besides, they'd been coming down here for months now. Nothing bad had ever happened during that time, and Scott seriously doubted that anything bad would ever happen here. Real life was just that boring.

He picked up a stone and skipped it across the body of water off to their scenic right.

"Why can't real life be like *Sky King*?" he asked. "I could fly a plane and catch robbers and stuff."

"Yeah, but then you'd have to deal with Penny," snorted Danny.

"Golly, you think so?" asked Scott in a condescending tone.

They both had a good laugh over their little joke. Scott and his best friend were only twelve, but they weren't stupid. They knew an annoying character when they saw one. There was always one in every show.

"Anyway, that's what I want to do," said Scott.

"What's that?" asked Danny.

"I want to fly like *Sky King*," replied Scott. "Be up in the air and see the ground from way up high. I bet everybody looks like ants that high up."

"I guess," shrugged Danny.

"There's no guess," said Scott unhappily. "That's what I want to do."

"I thought you wanted to swim or something," said Danny.

"Swimming's not a job," said Scott. "Whoever heard of swimming being a job? Nobody says, 'I wanna swim when I grow up.' That's just stupid."

"But you can swim better than anyone," said Danny. "You can hold your breath for four minutes while swimming."

"Yeah, but—" began Scott.

He heard them before he actually saw them. There were three of them, Gary Beans, Joey Foxworth, and Mason Duncan. These were older boys, Gary being the oldest at sixteen. They were pieces of townie trash as far as Scott was concerned, bullies and troublemakers that made everyone living here look bad.

These three had come out of the woods on Scott's left. They'd obviously been there the whole time, but Scott had been lost in his own thoughts, and Danny hadn't noticed them either.

Gary Beans walked up to them, took a drag off of the cigarette he was smoking, and then flicked the lit smoke at Scott's Buster Browns.

Scott danced a little backwards, careful not to slip and fall. He did not want to somehow pitch into the cold black of Prisoner's Creek.

"Did I hear that right?" asked Gary. "Did you say he can hold his breath for four minutes while swimming?"

"Y…Yeah…" stammered Danny.

Danny was a good friend, but he was also a coward; understandable, of course, considering how pudgy he was. Scott, on the other hand, was not afraid of these jackals.

The three teens menacing them immediately laughed in response to Danny's accurate description of Scott's swimming skills. Scott really could hold his breath for that long while swimming, but he sure as heck didn't want these jerks to know that.

He shot Danny an irritated look, but Danny wasn't even paying attention to him. His pudgy friend was as white as a wedding gown, a look of obvious fear plastered all over his round face.

"What a little liar," chuckled Gary Beans. "Nobody can hold their breath that long. Some little kid sure as hell can't do it."

"I can, too," scowled Scott. "I'm the best swimmer in town."

"Is that right?" asked Gary. "Why don't you prove it, little man."

"I don't have to prove nothin' to you," said Scott.

The three older boys laughed again as Gary shook his head in reply. He had a wicked grin on him, a sure sign he was up to no good.

"This kid's got an attitude, boys," said Gary. "This curtain climber thinks he can swim. Even worse, he thinks he can shoot off his mouth at his elders. No…you ain't much older than when your momma shot you out."

The older boys laughed again, and Mason Duncan, a tall and skinny redhead, elbow-nudged Gary in the side.

"His mom is stacked," nodded the redhead.

He cupped his hands under his chest and motioned them up and down.

"She's a real jiggler," grinned Mason.

"Is that right?" asked Gary. "I could squeeze that juice then."

Scott did not like the sound of that. It was one thing to harass a couple of kids minding their own business, but it really wasn't right to insult someone's mom. That was just plain wrong.

"Don't you talk about my mom that way!" yelled Scott. "I'll give you a knuckle sandwich, you no good punk!"

The change in attitude for the three teens was instantaneous, a Jekyll-and-Hyde transformation within the span of a second.

Gary pulled forth a sliver of black from his grey slacks and flicked a button on the side, and out popped the glint of steel in the afternoon sun. He bared the switchblade like a rogue fang, a fang ready to tear into an unprotected throat.

This actually startled Scott. He'd known these three were bad, but he hadn't known they were *this* bad.

He backed away a bit, and his first instinct was to run, but running wasn't swimming, and he didn't think he was fast enough to outpace them. Plus, he couldn't just abandon Danny. Danny was way too slow to ever outrun these punks.

"Grab the fat one," ordered Gary.

The two other boys, Joey and Mason, grabbed Danny, but Scott's best friend was too scared to even squeak…He just shook in place.

The two older boys stood on each side of Danny and held one of his arms, respectively.

"Leave him alone!" yelled Scott.

Gary brandished his deadly blade in front of Scott's face, but Scott backed up a bit more.

"You don't give me orders, squirt," growled the teen.

The older boy moved the tip of his blade up toward Danny's pudgy face until it rested underneath the younger boy's left eye. Danny's breath picked up in ragged bursts, but to his credit, he did not cry out.

Gary turned his attention back upon Scott and gave him a menacing stare.

"Now we'll see if you can hold your breath for four minutes," said the hostile punk. "'Cause if you don't, I'm going to pop his squinty little eye out of his fat head."

"No, you won't, you…" said Scott, but his voice trailed off as Gary put pressure on the blade.

Danny began to whine in a high-pitched tone, so Scott did not finish the insult he was about to say.

"Now…" continued Gary. "You are going to strip down and swim, you little zygote."

"I…I…uhhh…" said Scott, but he was at a loss for words.

Gary head-motioned toward Prisoner's Creek, and Scott looked out over the water in subconscious obedience.

"Out there is Prisoner's Rock," said Gary. "You're gonna swim out there."

Scott was well familiar with Prisoner's Rock; everyone was. It was a large chunk of boulder-like land just jutting out of Prisoner's Creek, but nobody ever went out to it. There were a lot of stories attached to it, or rather, a lot of stories attached to what was next to it, submerged next to it under the water. Nevertheless, Scott wasn't scared of some stupid local legends.

"That ain't nothin'," he said with what bravado he could muster. "Anyone can swim to that. The water's not even moving today."

Gary leaned forward and shone him a wicked grin.

"Yeah…but you ain't swimming to the rock, squirt," he said in a hushed voice.

"Oh, yeah?" asked Scott in a defiant tone.

"Yeah," replied Gary. "You're gonna swim past it, and then you're gonna swim down till you hit the bus doors."

Scott's heart leapt in his chest in spite of his bravery.

"Th…There ain't no bus," he said in a shaky voice.

"Oh, you know that bus is there," grinned Gary. "You can see the corner of it from the other bank…Oh, yeah. It's there."

"Then why hasn't anyone fished it up?" asked Scott.

"Why bother?" asked Gary. "Who wants to fish up that rusted hunk a junk?...Doesn't matter. You're gonna swim out there, swim through the doors, and dive down to the back of the bus."

He turned and pushed the flat of his blade into Danny's soft and squishy flesh again. The pudgy boy began to whine, but there was nothing Scott could do about it.

"'Cause if you don't, fat boy, here, is going to lose his depth perception," warned Gary.

"E…Even if there is a bus, you can't see it from here," said Scott. "It's easy for me to just swim out there and come right back. I could just tell you I found it. You wouldn't even know if I'd done it or not."

The three bullies all laughed in tandem.

"You're kind of stupid, ain't chya?" asked Gary. "You just keep shooting off your mouth, barking like a little dog…You see, I wasn't finished, you little anchovy. You're gonna swim down, find a way into that bus, and then you're gonna swim down in it. You're gonna bring back something that's proof that you were in that bus, or I'm gonna stick me a pig…Ain't that right, piggy?"

Gary pushed the flat of his blade back into Danny's soft cheek, just underneath Danny's left eye. Danny whined again, so Scott had no choice but to relent. Nevertheless, he was not going to relent in every way. These punks had to be defied one way or another.

"I'm not scared of swimming out there," said Scott in his bravest tone.

"Oh, yeah?" asked Gary. "Tell him, Joey. You're the historian."

Joey Foxworth, a big kid with broad shoulders, nodded and gave Scott a sinister grin.

"This is Duggan's River, though it's not big enough to be a real river," said Joey. "Everybody calls it Prisoner's Creek because of what happened twenty-one years ago."

"That's just a story…" said Scott, but he wasn't so sure.

"Not a story," said Joey as he shook his head no. "It's true. That prison bus slid off the road up yonder during a heavy storm, went crashing through the brush on the other side of the creek, and pitched right into the water here. It happened July 1st, 1931."

"Yeah, and all the prisoners got out except one," said Gary.

"William Parsey," nodded Joey in strange understanding.

"They called him Raging Bill Parsey in prison," grinned Gary. "Pickaxe Parsey is what they called him before he got sentenced. Killed a man with a pickaxe…He was the worst one on that bus. Even the other prisoners were scared of him."

"Yeah," said Joey. "It's said a general store owner cheated him out of ten dollars, and you don't steal from Bill Parsey. The owner used that ten for change. Parsey found the guy who had his ten dollars and killed him even though he wasn't the one that took it…killed him dead with a pickaxe. He even killed a man in prison for stealing his dinner roll. Bashed his brains in on the prison floor."

"He was a real killer all right," grinned Gary. "A real killer. You don't steal from Bill Parsey, and if you do, you better ditch whatever you stole fast."

"The only thing he was allowed to keep on him was a silver dollar," continued Joey. "It was a 1910 silver dollar. There weren't any silver dollars minted in 1931 because of the Great Depression, so Parsey held onto the one he had."

"He was gonna carry it with him to the chair," said Gary. "He thought he could buy his way out of Hell with it."

"Yeah," said Joey. "One time, a guy in prison stole that dollar and used it to trade for some smokes. Parsey didn't kill the thief, no. He just killed the guy who had the dollar. That thief never stole anything again…He was too scared to…so you don't steal from Bill Parsey…

"Yeah, he wasn't chained with the others when the bus crashed. He was chained to his own seat for everyone's safety, and everyone else just left him there. They didn't bother to unchain him."

"That's right, squirt," smirked Gary. "He's still down there, rotting away."

"I don't believe that…" said Scott, but once again, he wasn't so sure.

Yeah, he'd heard the stories…the bus was cursed, it was haunted, blah, blah, blah, but he'd never heard of any "Bill Parsey."

"Oh, he's down there," said Gary. "Now…you're gonna swim out to Prisoner's Rock, dive down till you hit the bus doors, swim in, and look for something to bring back as proof that you were down there…Got it?"

"What if there's nothing down there?" asked Scott.

"Then fat boy, here, loses an eye," grinned Gary.

"If you can hold your breath for four minutes," nodded Joey, "then that's about two minutes while swimming."

"Yeah, yeah…" nodded Gary in return. "That should be more than enough time to find something, tough guy. That's if you're not *chicken.*"

Scott did not want to swim in that dark, muddy water. For one thing, there was no light down there, just the rays shining down from the sun to light his way. Plus, that bus…Even so, he wasn't going to abandon his friend like these no-good punks would their own. He knew better.

He made his decision then and there. He was going to teach these cowards a lesson. Bullies were cowards that only picked on the small and the weak, and he knew this; everybody did.

Scott took off his shirt and then unbuckled his belt.

"Okay," he said firmly, no fear in his voice. "I ain't chicken. I don't believe there's any Bill Parsey. You just made that up…I'll be back with something, just you wait."

The three older boys laughed again, and even Gary removed his blade from Danny's chubby cheek as he shook his own head.

"Yeah, let's see you do it," chuckled Gary. "Say hi to Bill for us."

"This baby can't make it," laughed Mason. "He'll turn his boxers yellow."

"I can, too," said Scott. "I'll be back with something...I'm not yellow, and I can swim better than anyone else in town, you'll see...It's made in the shade."

The three bullies laughed again as Scott stripped down to his boxer shorts. He nodded once toward Danny in confidence, and then he stepped into the water.

The water of Prisoner's Creek was slow today and slightly cold despite the bright sun above. Nevertheless, Danny was depending on him, so he waded forward until he was swimming, and that did not take long. Prisoner's Creek was far deeper than it appeared to be from the banks, especially around Prisoner's Rock.

The distance to Prisoner's Rock took him a little longer than expected, mainly because the water grew colder the closer he got to the rounded boulder jutting up from the middle of this mini-river. Even so, he didn't have to hold his breath yet. His plan was to climb onto the rock or try to, walk over to the other side of the rock where the supposed bus was, and lower himself into the water from there.

He reached the slick sides of Prisoner's Rock, but the surface facing the sun was just dry, rough stone, so it was not as difficult as he had thought it was going to be to pull himself up and onto that dry surface.

Scott stood up on the large boulder sticking up from Prisoner's Creek, adjusted his boxers, and turned to look back toward the bank he'd just left. They were still there, the three obnoxious, hostile bullies, and of course, Danny, whose fear was tangible, even if it wasn't visible on his fat face from this distance.

Scott nodded once toward Danny and then turned to get back to the task at hand. He still had to get something as evidence that he had entered the so-called bus that was supposed to be under the water here, a proof that he could actually hold his breath as long as he had said he could and, of course, a proof that he wasn't yellow.

He walked to the other side of Prisoner's Rock, and the surface of the stone was hot on his bare feet. The only thing saving him from burns was the fact that the soles of his feet were still wet.

He walked to the edge of the rock and stared down into the dark water below. There was a corner of something metal protruding from the water, a rounded and rusted corner of something, but if it were part of a bus, he did not know.

"Time to find out," he said to himself.

He lowered himself into the water and felt his bare feet touch rusted metal. There was something here, and it did feel like the roof of a vehicle, but he wouldn't know for sure until he took a closer look.

He swam around to the corner of this submerged vehicle and held onto the rounded rusted metal of the protruding piece. He could see a darkness below him, a rectangular opening of shadow that could only be the open doors of the submerged bus.

"Well, I'll be," he breathed out. "There is a bus here…but I don't believe in any Bill Parsey."

Still, there was that doubt in his mind, that doubt that was always in the hearts of young boys when it came to danger.

"No," said Scott to himself. "Let's just go in and grab something. We'll do it quick."

He breathed in while pushing his stomach out in order to fill his lungs to maximum capacity. He dove down through the open doors a second later and entered the bus interior.

There should have been no light down here, nothing to guide his way, but there actually was a light, a strange emerald glow coming from deep down, deep,

deep down at the back of the bus. The back of this long vehicle had to be settled on the riverbed, so there should definitely not have been any light, but it was there…He could see it.

He swam down toward the light. He was curious now. He had learned in school about fish that glowed in the dark, but all of those kinds of fish were ocean fish. They weren't freshwater fish. Still, he wanted to know what was glowing down there; he wanted to see what was making that light.

The eerie green light below lit up the outlines of bare seats long stripped of their covers, those metal seats long rusted out and eaten away by time.

Scott pushed his way down toward the light, swimming down and down like some overgrown frog headed toward the bottom of a murky pond. The light glowed brighter as the water grew colder and the pressure increased, a bright green and macabre glow that shone even through this pitch black.

At this point, he could grab whatever, a screw, a spring, whatever, but he was curious about the light beneath him. He had to grab the tops of rusty seats to pull himself down, and his time had almost been a minute gone, a strain on his lungs considering the strain he was putting on his own muscles.

He reached the last two seats at the back of the bus, the last two seats parked in an eternal cockeyed position directly over the riverbed.

His eyes widened out of reflex. He was used to swimming in fresh water with his eyes open, something a lot of other boys wouldn't do, but he preferred to see where he was going when down below, even if it was dark underwater ninety percent of the time.

His eyes had widened because of the skeletal figure at the bottom of the bus, the bones in scraps of weathered rags, the bones that sat in a grinning position staring up with hollow sockets for the rest of eternity.

He did not scream. Scott refused to scream underwater. Maybe he would have above the waterline, but he knew better than to open his mouth down here, certainly not down this deep.

The green glow, that ghastly color, was coming from a small flat disk, and that disk was positioned in what was left of this corpse's skeletal right hand.

Scott could see the rusted chains and bracelets locking this body to the seat, a final resting place for what was supposed to be an imaginary boogeyman.

He bolted out of there, shooting up like a rocket back toward the open doors of the bus. He had no business being down here. Besides, he was feeling the serious burn of lack of oxygen in his lungs, and he needed to breathe.

It took him far less time to reach the top of the bus, far less time than swimming down, though swimming upwards was a strenuous workout on every one of his muscles.

He reached the opened doors, pulled himself through, and took in a deep and gasping breath after he breached the surface.

He shook his head free of water for a second and took in some more breaths.

What he had just seen was crazy, incredible, and also terrifying, but he had seen it, and only he had seen it. No one else knew about it, at least, he had never heard of anyone who had confirmed the Bill Parsey story. In fact, he had never even heard of Bill Parsey until Joey had spoken the man's name for the first time. It was incredible that he now knew something no one else did…but still, that glow…

"That's g…got to be it," he said through chattering breaths. "That's got t…to be his silver dollar."

It appeared that Bill Parsey still had his silver dollar, but why it was glowing and why it was glowing green did not make sense to Scott. He had heard in school from Jimmy Calloway that radiation glowed green, so maybe the dollar had gone radioactive. Whatever the case, he could see it, and if he could see it, he could grab it.

Of course, he did not like the idea of that corpse being down there, but Bill Parsey was long dead, twenty-one years gone, so that didn't really matter, and he had to tell himself that a few times to get the courage to dive once more. He'd never seen a real dead body before, but his best friend, Danny, was on the line, so that body was nothing compared to that.

"Let's j…just do it," he nodded to himself. "We'll get that silver dollar…It's the atomic age, after all. Things can go radioactive. That dollar's got t…to be radioactive. It went radioactive somehow. That must be why it's glowing."

He nodded to himself once more in confidence of his own strange kid-logic. This was all the courage he needed to go back down there, get that silver dollar, and save Danny.

He pushed out his stomach and filled his lungs to maximum capacity once more. He was going to go get that dollar.

He dove down into the black once again, entering the open doors of the bus, pushing himself through and down, down toward the glowing of the silver dollar at the back of the submerged bus, that back end resting at the bottom of the riverbed.

The water was cold, a chill that sank deep into his twelve-year-old bones, but he grabbed the seat tops, pulled his body forward, and swam his way down toward the green-glowing dollar and its former owner, what remained of Bill Parsey.

The trip down was a strain on his lungs. He could hold his breath for four minutes straight, and he could hold it for two minutes with normal swimming, but this diving was strenuous, more exertion on his muscles than he was used to, so he did not know how long he could safely be down here, and that length of time was not long if he was correct in the estimation of his own limits.

There was also the pressure. The pressure on his ears was beginning to hurt, and he did not like that at all. He was used to this kind of pressure due to his previous and abundant swimming, but that didn't mean he liked it.

He pushed himself toward the light, that dismal and eerie glow emanating from the prize he sought. He stopped before the grinning skeletal corpse of Bill Parsey, reached forward, and snatched the glowing coin from the open fingerbones of the long dead murderer. He pinched the coin between his right index finger and his right thumb; he needed its glow as a light source to find his way back up.

Scott immediately turned to swim back up. He was not sticking around here, even if he could have held his breath for longer. However, he did not get the chance to swim up as planned, no…No, the struggle had begun.

The long-withered and skeletal corpse of Bill Parsey reached forward, the rusted chains snapping free from his chair, the malignant and bony digits of his right hand reaching forward to close upon Scott's left ankle.

Scott turned upon feeling the icy and terrible touch of that long-dead murderer. He could see the grinning skull in the green limelight, the awful, bony fingers wrapped around his left ankle, and he wanted to scream, but he had long since trained himself not to. No, his eyes widened in response as he tried to swim up, but Parsey's other skeletal hand grabbed onto the rusted metal top of the seat in front of his own withered corpse, firmly locking the both of them in place.

Scott was all panic now. There was nothing to say in his mind about it; it was simply a brutal fight for survival. He kicked and struggled to get free, but the icy grip around his left ankle was too strong, the bony digits digging into his skin with a freezing doom.

He felt his lungs burning from exertion. He was running out of air, and fast. He had to breathe, and he wasn't even sure if he could make it back to the surface at this point, but he had to try…First, though…he needed to get free.

He placed his free left hand on the glass of a tiny window that was higher up than could be easily accessed, a small window that had somehow miraculously survived twenty-one years of submersion and overhead storms. He pushed hard on the glass and struggled wildly, but to no avail. The icy grip buried in his skin was too strong, too powerful, but there had to be a way to free himself. There had to be.

He was almost out of air, almost to his bursting point, but he wasn't about to give up. He would never do that. He was not going to die down here with the skeletal corpse of Bill Parsey, dying down here with nothing but an oily handprint on a long-forgotten prison-bus window.

It came to him in a flash of desperate inspiration. No, Scott wasn't yellow, and he sure as heck wasn't stupid. He had something he could try, probably the last chance he was ever going to have down here.

He momentarily stopped his struggling, turned, and held up the glowing coin in front of Bill Parsey's hollowed-out eye sockets, holding it up as if to say, "Take it."

The ragged, skeletal corpse did not let go of him, but it did let go of the top of the seat it had been holding onto. That empty left hand reached forward to snatch at the coin, but Scott used that fateful moment to kick up into Parsey's bony, spindly right arm, kicking up and into the bones of Parsey's wrist with his right foot.

Parsey's skeletal fingers popped free, and Scott rocketed upwards without a second's hesitation.

His lungs were about to burst, but he shot upwards, swimming with all his might. He hit the open doors at the top of the bus, his glowing prize still pinched in his right fingers.

He made the unfortunate mistake of peering back down into the depths beneath him, and the green glow of the silver dollar revealed Parsey shooting up after him, that skull grinning, those hollow eye sockets empty and yet full of hate.

Scott did not stop just to breathe. He did not have that kind of time. He breached the surface of the water and struggled to pull himself up onto Prisoner's Rock instead. He took in deep gasps of air as he pulled himself up on that hot stone surface baking in the sun, but he did not even stop there. He dashed across the hot surface and splashed back into the water seconds later, intent on swimming back to the bank with everything he had left.

He took a brief moment to pop the silver dollar into his mouth, freeing up his hands, and then he swam like he had never swum before.

Scott knew Parsey was behind him, right there under the water, right behind him, so he did not slow down. What he was going to do once he hit the bank, once he was on land, was another story, but he'd cross that bridge when he came to it.

He swam to shore and dashed onto dry land and scrub grass as quickly as he could. He stopped for a moment, spit the coin into the palm of his right hand, held his knees, and took in some deep breaths. He was exhausted, and with good reason.

The first thing he did after that, however, was put some distance between himself and the water, a good ten feet. He did not want Parsey grabbing him again from out of that cold black.

"So, the little curtain climber made it back," snorted Gary. "So, what'd you get, squirt?"

Scott took in a few more breaths before addressing this obnoxious bully. He wasn't afraid of Gary anymore. He wasn't afraid of any of them. He'd already faced a real murderer, a murderer that had risen from beyond the grave, and these three punks weren't even close to that kind of a threat.

He opened the palm of his right hand and displayed the silver dollar. The dollar was no longer glowing, but there it was, gleaming in the sunlight, pristine and untouched by time as if newly minted.

"What the…?" began Gary.

The older boy snatched the dollar out of Scott's hand and held it up for everyone to see.

"There…it is…" gasped Scott. "Bill Parsey's silver dollar…"

"That's some bullsh…" began Gary, but his voice trailed off as he studied the coin between his fingers.

"It says 1910," he said in audible disbelief. "But that's impossible…This thing should be tarnished to hell and gone by now…"

"The bus was there, and I swam to the…the bottom of it," nodded Scott. "I took it from Parsey's…own hand. He was…was down there, like you said, chained to his seat. I took it right from him…I told you I wasn't yellow."

"You're full of it," said Gary, but there were cracks in his own statement, a disbelief that crept through to the surface of his voice.

"That's his dollar," said Scott, this time with a firmness of belief that countered anything Gary had to say.

Nevertheless, he wasn't stupid. He knew what to do now, even if he had to lie a little.

"I've heard that certain minerals on the bottoms of riverbeds and creeks can keep a dollar like that from tarnishing," he nodded. "They come out looking new, unlike stuff they find in oceans, because seas and oceans are saltwater, but freshwater beds like Prisoner's Creek keep them nice and shiny…Don't take my word for it, though…Joey knows…Ask him."

Gary turned his suspicious gaze upon his more knowledgeable companion.

"Is that true?" he asked.

Joey gave him a sheepish grin, shrugged, and then proceeded to give Gary an uncertain half-nod.

"It must be," he said nervously. "I mean, look at it. It's got to be Parsey's. It's a 1910 silver dollar. Heck, a museum would pay big money for that…"

Gary nodded, immediately stuffed the dollar into the right pocket of his grey slacks, and gave Scott a warning glare.

"I guess you're not such a little yellow baby after all," he frowned. "You can swim, I'll give you that…but I don't want to see you or your fat friend around here again. This is our spot, got it?"

Scott nodded, snatched up his clothes and shoes, and motioned for Danny to get moving. He could put his clothes back on once they'd made tracks. He was not about to stick around here.

They made some distance between the older boys as they walked into the woods and back toward town. Scott felt better now that those three punks were out of their hair, far better now that they were away from Prisoner's Creek in general, and he was also relieved that both he and Danny were safe.

They were silent for a few minutes of trudging before Danny spoke up with a question.

"Did you really find that bus?" asked the chubby boy.

"Yep," said Scott.

He stopped to put his clothes back on. They were far enough away from Prisoner's Creek now that he wasn't worried about those three bullies anymore…or the creek itself.

"Did you really find Bill Parsey?" asked Danny.

"Yep," said Scott.

"Then we need to tell someone that Gary stole your silver dollar," said Danny.

"Nope," said Scott with a shake of his head.

"Why not?" asked Danny. "He threatened us both, and he has a switchblade. He should be in jail. He was going to carve out my eye. You know he's going to end up killing someone…He should really be in jail."

"Doesn't matter," said Scott firmly. "He won't be around much longer. We won't have to worry about Gary Beans anymore."

"What?" asked Danny. "What do you mean by that? Why won't we have to worry?"

"Because you don't steal from Bill Parsey," said Scott.

He gave Danny a look that could freeze juice into a popsicle, and then he lifted his left pants leg.

Danny's eyes goggled out of his doughy face as he stared down at the four, long, skeletal, purple bruises wrapped around Scott's left ankle, the shorter thumb bruise topping off that macabre injury.

*****

Gary finished brushing his teeth as he spit into his bathroom sink. The second-floor hallway light was on outside his bedroom door, but his bedroom light was off, just like he liked it. He was no baby that needed a nightlight, but he did need some light in order to see around in case he had to get up for something.

He was dressed in his white PJs with the red stripes, and he was ready for bed, though he wasn't necessarily ready for sleep.

He cleaned off his toothbrush and set it back in its little porcelain bowl. He picked up the silver dollar he had set on the side of the sink and flipped it once, catching it as it came down. It was his now, and he was going to be famous for it. He was going to make a cool mint from this, even be in the local paper. Maybe he could even get a spot on TV…

"That little zygote actually did me a favor," he snorted. "That means I won't have to kill him yet."

He stepped into the darkness of his bedroom and stopped at the sight of his open bedroom door.

"I didn't leave that op…" he began, but his voice trailed off as he stared at the wet, muddy prints upon the bare wood of his bedroom floor.

They were muddy prints of toes and feet leading into his bedroom from the hallway, but not fully formed, almost like…

He stared down at the silver dollar in his right hand as the shiny coin began to glow a green light, subtle at first, and then strong and bright mere seconds later.

"What the—" he began, but he was cut short by a creaking noise behind him.

He turned toward the inner darkness of his room and screamed as a rusty pickaxe came speeding toward his thoroughly shocked and surprised face.

About the Author

Mr. Marlott has a background in psychology and classic literature, and he enjoys literature of all types and genres. Mr. Marlott lives somewhere within the United States, has two Gen-Z children, and enjoys telling stories to anyone who will listen.

Books and Sites

You can read new stories of mine for free at bloodytwine.com. This site is my workshop where I work on new stories and perfect them for publication.

For more twisted tales with twisted endings, you can purchase *Bloody Twine #1* and *Bloody Twine #2* wherever they are sold.

If you want the basic building blocks to writing genre fiction, you can explore my two cents on the subject in *The Quick and Easy Guide to Writing Genre Fiction*.

For great cosmic horror, you can read some awesome eldritch-horror tales by Bert S. Lechner. You can purchase Mr. Lechner's collection of cosmic horror, *The Roots Grow into the Earth*, wherever it is sold. You can also check out Mr. Lechner's personal website at bertwriteshorror.com.

For a mix of traditional horror and cosmic horror, check out some incredible short stories by James Dermond. You can purchase Mr. Dermond's Doorways to the Unseen series wherever it is sold. You can also visit Mr. Dermond's website at jamesdermond.com.

If you like this book, give it a good review and tell me what your favorite story was in this bundle.

THE BLOODY TWINE SERIES

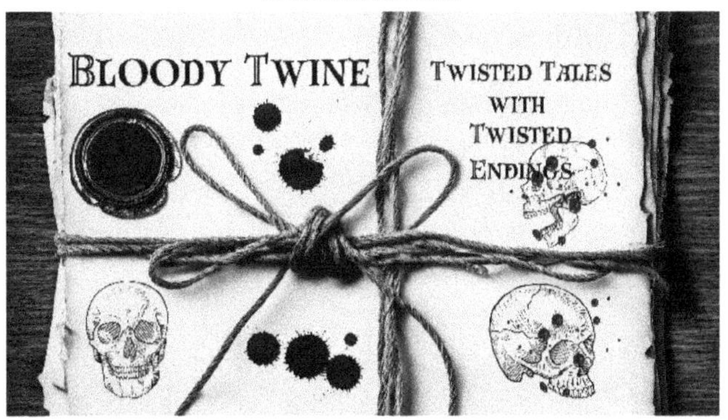

𝕎elcome to the Bloody Twine Series, a collection of short horror stories written specifically for horror fans everywhere. These books contain a minimum of 10 traditional short horror stories for the collections and a minimum of 5 traditional short horror stories for the selections, all for your terrifying entertainment, so go someplace quiet, dim the lights, sit back, and enjoy some twisted tales with twisted endings.

Imagine walking into an abandoned storage room filled with old newspapers and magazines, all articles stacked in bundles neatly tied with twine, but then you discover other bundles, bundles not so neatly tied, ragged bundles of yellowed and partially-charred paper tied in bloodstained twine.

You see, some stories are meant to educate, and some stories are meant to entertain, but some stories…some stories are simply looking for a victim.

Enjoy.

Matthew L. Marlott

THE QUICK AND EASY GUIDE TO WRITING GENRE FICTION

Thinking of writing your own tale of love, redemption, and heroics? Writing genre fiction is an art, and *The Quick and Easy Guide to Writing Genre Fiction* provides the building blocks for being successful in this art. Learn all of the necessary techniques to get yourself started with writing in your chosen genre. Whether you're writing a mystery, a romance, a thriller, science-fiction, horror, fantasy, or any other genre, you'll have the foundation for writing great stories right here at your fingertips in this guide.

Included in this guide is a step-by-step instruction of what it takes to put together your creation in any genre. Also included in this guide is the complete creation process of an original short story by author Matthew L. Marlott, so you, too, can have an easy example of how to create your own stories, whether those stories are short stories, novels, or novellas. You'll be able to create your own worlds and your own universes, so learn the basics of writing genre fiction for the purpose of selling, for publication on a site, for fanfiction, or just for your own personal satisfaction.

Remember, if you want real life, you can just walk out the front door. Why not write down your own story on paper or screen instead? Get started with your journey into genre fiction by learning from this invaluable guide. Don't wait until you're on your deathbed. Get started today.

Matthew L. Marlott

THE ROOTS GROW INTO THE EARTH

"In the dark we found them…"

The Roots grow into the Earth. Unseen conduits of Power, growing through the darkness of the void; walkways for malevolent, eldritch things to travel, connecting their dead worlds to ours.

In this collection of nine short stories and novelettes, you will find tales of unfathomable predators, cosmic gods, dark magic, and the people who cross their path: from archaeologists, long on the search for the find of the century, ensnared by a being beyond their understanding, to a man who notices a detail on a wall in his house for the first time, unwittingly inviting the attention of a malefic force from beyond the stars.

The Roots Grow Into the Earth consists of nine of Bert S. Lechner's previously published works, including three stories available as standalone eBooks: Interstate, the Wall, and Joanne's Vault.

Bert S. Lechner

DOORWAYS TO THE UNSEEN

"The Doorways to the Unseen series is a collection of short story books from author James Dermond. The stories take the reader around the world and through time, with each tale offering a glimpse into a supernatural episode. Every volume in the series contains six short horror stories meant to chill the blood and inspire unimaginable terror in their readers.

"So, step inside and find that which has been hidden from you all along. Where the unknown and the unimaginable meet."

James Dermond

Bloody Twine #3
Twisted Tales with Twisted Endings
Copyright 1st ed. © 2024 Matthew L. Marlott

9 798989 444458